Loving
THE SAVAGE
IN HIM

A Twisted Love Story

A NOVEL BY

CANDY MOORE

© 2017

Published by Royalty Publishing House

www.royaltypublishinghouse.com

ALL RIGHTS RESERVED

Contains explicit language & adult themes suitable for ages 16+

CHAPTER 1

I was sitting in the hospital room, holding onto my mother's hand as she lay with her eyes closed. She just had Chemotherapy for the second time in two and a half weeks. The procedure always left her feeling exhausted.

My name is Shauntel Harris. I'm a college student at Spelman, majoring in education studies. I'm nineteen years old but on days like this, I feel damn near thirty! I live in Atlanta with my sickly mother who is battling breast cancer. I'm the only child to my now deceased father, who passed away two years ago from a massive heart attack, and my mother who lost her left breast a year ago to cancer. It had gone into remission. But two months ago, on her routine doctor's visit, she found out that the cancer was in her right breast.

I exhaled a sigh of distress and exhaustion as I rubbed her hands while she tried to regain her strength. I was feeling defeated. My father left us an adequate amount of money in his will. He used to work as a civil engineer at an oil company. But with my mother's medical expenses, my college tuition, and our daily survival expenses, the money was disappearing faster than weed at Snoop's house!

"Mom," I said softly as I squeezed her hands.

Her eyelids fluttered briefly before she slowly opened her chestnut, brown eyes and focused them on me. She gave me a weak smile.

"I have to go to work now. Are you going to be OK?" I asked, but not really wanting to leave her. However, I was trying my best to get my money right so that we wouldn't end up having nothing at all.

"Baby, don't you worry about me. You go on to work. I don't even know why you're working; your father left us more than enough money to get us by Shaunie," she said, using the nickname that my dad gave me when I was a baby.

I honestly didn't have the heart to tell her that we were barely staying afloat. After I pay the remainder of her medical bills and my tuition payment, we'll almost be broke!

"Mom, you know I gotta' keep active when I'm not in school, or I'll go crazy," I said, which was stretching the truth. I feigned a smile as I got up, collected my things, and prepared to leave.

"I'll be back after my shift to take you home, OK? I love you," I told her as I kissed her forehead.

"I love you too, baby." As soon as those words passed her lips, she instantly closed her eyes as if speaking was too tiring for her.

I walked to the door and stood for a while as I watched her chest rise and fall. I assumed that she'd drifted to sleep. As the tears formed, I began walking down the corridor and made my way to the front entrance.

If my mother died, I'd be so lost. I had no idea what I'd do with myself. I was such a loner; I barely had any friends, and I definitely had no boyfriend. I didn't have any time to date! All my time was spent attending classes. When I wasn't doing that, I worked as a cashier in a local coffee shop. And when I wasn't doing that, I was taking care of my mother. So, basically . . . I had no life!

I walked out of Piedmont Hospital towards the parking lot to my 2013 plum purple Toyota Camry. It wasn't flashy like the vehicles that some of students drove at college, but it got me from point A to point B.

As I pulled out of the hospital and drove towards the coffee shop, I thought of ways that I could make extra cash on the side. *I could probably braid hair. I was pretty good at it. Besides, I see some women in my class with jacked up braids,* I thought while stopped at a traffic light.

My phone began ringing. I reached for my handbag on the passenger side to retrieve my phone. When I looked at the screen, I saw that it was my work number. I was about to answer when the driver in the car behind me honked their horn. I didn't realize that the light had turned green. As I pulled out to continue driving on Collier Road, a black Range Rover came pummeling in my direction from the side street, Wycliff Road.

"Shit!" I screamed out in shock.

While stunned and panicked, I tried to avoid the side of my car from being crashed into. I pulled my steering wheel to the extreme left, climbed the curb, and came to an abrupt stop. I sat in my car, said a prayer, and held my chest because my heart was beating hard enough to pop out of it. That asshole in the Range Rover almost killed my ass. I looked up to see the driver pull over to the side of the road and climb out his vehicle.

1

As I watched him walking to my car, I suddenly found that I could barely breathe. Not from the accident, but from the fine man that was slowly approaching me. This brother was foine! He was light skinned, about 5' 7", and built like a Greek god! He was dressed in workout apparel like he'd just come from working out at the gym. He was wearing a red vest, that was cut low on the sides, with the word, "BEAST" written in white on the front. He also wore gray sweatpants and red and white Jordan's.

He had tattoos of stars almost entirely covering his muscled right arm. His face was clean shaven and he was sporting a low fade. He had the most wonderful pair of light brown eyes. However, the closer he got, the more pissed I saw his facial expression become.

I sat waiting. I was still shaken up and unable to move as he arrived at my car and forcefully pulled my door handle to open the door. I couldn't do anything but sit. I'm sure I had a shocked and slightly scared look on my face as he pounded on my window.

"Yo! What the fuck! How the fuck did you get your license?" he screamed and continued pounding on my window. I wasn't sure if I should get out my car or lower my window; this was no timid or average-looking nigga. His muscles intimidated the fuck out of me!

"Don't you hear me talking to you? Man, open this mothafuckin' door!" he shouted as he hit his palms against my window and tugged on the door handle again.

I unlocked the door and cautiously got out the car. I looked at the way his eyes roamed over my body, and I swear I could see him start to calm down. I was 5' 5" with a smooth, cinnamon complexion. I was in between slim and thick with mad curves and a firm, round ass. I was no Nicki Minaj, but my ass was the right size. I had my hair in a messy bun. I rarely wore weave as my hair was naturally shoulder length. I had my mother's chestnut-colored eyes.

I pulled on my denim skirt because I suddenly felt that it was a couple sizes too short as his gaze roamed over my exposed upper thighs. My 38C breasts hugged the plain white Polo tee that I wore, which had the logo of the coffee shop that I worked at.

"Well, that's a nice attitude for someone who damn near killed my ass!" I said to him as I folded my arms. The nerve of this asshole to be angry at me after he pulled into the street when his light was red. My light was green; therefore, I was in the right.

"The fuck you mean! Your light was red, not mine, shawty. You better get your eyes checked," he stated as he made his way around my car and checked it out.

"Your attitude is as nasty as the words coming outta' your mouth. Get the hell out my way. I'm already late for work." I made a quick scan of my car and sucked my teeth as I noticed the passenger mirror had been hit. "Look what the fuck you did to my mirror, I can't afford to get this shit fixed!" I exclaimed and then let out an exasperated sigh while placing my hands to the top of my head.

"Look who's talking about foul mouth! Don't you hear the words coming out your own mouth? Chill, aight. I'll take care of it. Gimme yo' number real quick. Where you work at?" he asked as he pulled his iPhone out his pocket and unlocked the screen.

He looked up at me, waiting for me to give my number. I just stared at his eyes, unable to say anything. Should I even bother? I was pretty sure he'd never call to help me get my mirror fixed. I started biting on my bottom lip as I contemplated what to do.

I should probably let my insurance cover it, but Lord knows how long that shit will take. I turned my attention back to him, and he was staring at the way I was biting on my lower lip, which made me stop abruptly.

"Are you sure you gon' call? I really can't afford to fix this right now," I said. I couldn't help but let my eyes roam over his hard muscles once more. I peeped at his ride. It looked like it could've been on an episode of that cheesy TV show "Pimp My Ride". It had chrome, 20" rims, all the handles were chrome, and the tint was so dark that you couldn't see shit but your own reflection. I heard the faint sound of music playing; it sounded like Young M.A.'s "OOOUUU".

"I got you. Tap your digits in my phone real quick," he said as he handed his phone to me.

I quickly registered my number and handed the phone back to him.

He looked at my number, then he looked at me and smiled. "Shauntel, huh? So, what time do you get off work, Ms. Shauntel?" he asked while smiling at me provocatively.

I felt my pussy twitch, and was slightly embarrassed.

"At 4:30," I replied like a robot. I don't know what it was about him, but the way my body was reacting to him bothered me----A LOT!

"Aight, shawty, don't worry about your mirror. I'll holla at you."

And with those words, he crossed the street and headed towards his Range Rover. That left me to gape at his toned, muscular back which was very visible because of the vest he wore. As he opened the door, the sound of music blaring filled my ears. This time, Fetty Wap's "Trap Queen" played:

I'm like hey, wassup hello

seen yo' pretty ass soon as you came in the door

I just wanna' chill, gotta stack for us to roll

Married to the money, introduced her to my stove

Showed her how to whip it, now she remix it for the low

She my trap queen, let her hit the bando.

I heard the words clearly before he closed his door. Turning to my car, I got in and prepared to leave. I took one last look at the Range before it drove off because I knew that I'd be the one fixing my own goddamn mirror. *That nigga thinks he's slick. He didn't even have the courtesy to give me his name!* I shook my head and took my late ass to work.

CHAPTER 2

*I*t was a busy day at the coffee shop. I kept checking the time because I knew that I had to be back at the hospital at 5:00 to pick my mom up. My co-worker, Cocoa, and I finally got some breathing space when business at the shop finally slowed down at 4:15, which was only fifteen minutes before to closing time. I began cleaning up and preparing to leave at 4:30 on the dot.

I was wiping the counters when Cocoa said, "You go on and get your moms. I'll lock up girl." She scratched her funky weave and smacked her gum loudly.

Cocoa was a nice person and all, but her attitude was ratchet as hell. She always wore those long ass Brazilian bundles that went all the way down to her fat ass. Her ass was so big that you could easily sit a full dining set on that thing. She was hella' thick with wide hips, but her waist and breasts were small. She had 32B cups. She was dark colored and had a pretty face with deep dimples. She drove all the niggas wild.

"You sure Cocoa? I don't mind helping you out," I said, but I'd already put the rag down so that I could grab my bag from behind the counter and leave. "Yeah, girl. I got this. Young B will be over in a few to pick me up. Go on ahead 'fore I change my mind," she said as she walked towards the table that I'd been cleaning to take over.

Just as I was making my way behind the counter, I heard my phone ringing inside my bag. I panicked a little, thinking that it might've been the hospital calling about my mom. I looked at the strange number and answered.

"Hello?" I said quietly.

"Where you work at, shawty?" A vaguely familiar voice filled my ear.

Even though I was pretty sure who it was, I still asked, "Who is this?" I waited for his answer and began biting my lower lip.

"You want your mirror fixed or nah? Give me the address so I can punch it in my GPS real quick."

I had to pull the phone away from my ear and look at it. *This nigga right here!* "Your unmannerly ass never even bothered to give me your name," I said, giving him attitude. Was his ass raised by wolves or some shit! I mean really.

"Oh, my bad, shawty. You coulda' just asked a nigga. It's Gucci Boss, he said. He dragged out his name for emphasis.

"Gucci Boss? Well, I know that ain't your government name," I said. I felt a smile tugging at the corner of my mouth.

Cocoa was suddenly in front of my face mouthing unspoken words that I couldn't make out.

"It's Jayceon. Tell me where you work at, damn, all these questions!"

I shook my head at his response before I rattled off where I worked. Jayceon said he'd be over in about ten minutes and then hung up.

"Bitch, how in the hell you know Gucci Boss?" Cocoa asked with her eyes wide.

What was wrong with her? Acting like I said it was August Alsina or some shit.

"That's the asshole that almost killed me this morning and made me late for work. Why? What's up?" I answered nonchalantly. I didn't even care if it was even the same person Cocoa was referring to.

"I know your stuck-up ass don't know anybody. But girl, that nigga run these streets out here, and his money is loud," Cocoa said

That left me a bit upset that she thought I was stuck up because I wasn't! "What'chu mean? What he does for a living?" I asked as I made myself a coffee. I took a sip and waited for her reply.

She laughed as if I'd said something funny. "Bitch, maybe if yo' ass wasn't so sheltered, you would know that he runs shit out here in the ATL. His street game is banging. Nigga got dope blocks on top of dope blocks on top of dope blocks! His money is as tall as you. Shit!"

I swallowed slowly as Cocoa described Jayceon to me. I mean, should I really be surprised? Most of these niggas out here in the ATL were dope boys. Personally, I didn't know any. I steered clear from those types. My father was so strict; he would've strung my ass up if he found out that I was entertaining company from any street niggas.

Secretly however, I'd always been a bit curious about what it'd be like to be with a 'thug'. I'd eavesdropped on many conversations in the bathroom at school where girls talked about being with guys from the streets. The flashy cars, the way they spoiled them with their bank rolls. Plus, the way they spoke about the sex! You would swear these niggas were some type of porn stars.

So, my curiosity was piqued, but I knew deep down that I'd never find out on my own. Who'd want an inexperienced, plain jane like myself?

"Oh yeah? Well, I just want him to fix my mirror, and he can be on his way. Why he call himself Gucci Boss, anyways?" I questioned Cocoa who continued cleaning the counters.

She laughed softly. "Oh, you'll see when he gets here." She shook her head as if me not knowing any type of details about this fool was a big deal. All I knew was that he tried to run me over with his Range.

"I'm about to use the bathroom real quick," I said. I put my coffee down, grabbed my handbag, and headed to the washroom. After I closed the door behind me, I walked to the mirror. I scared my own goddamn self when I saw my reflection. I quickly searched my handbag and pulled out my brush. When I untied my hair, it fell in a long cascade just below my shoulders. I brushed it lightly, then put it in a high ponytail. I grabbed my MAC powder and dipped my makeup brush in to take the shine off my face. Next, I applied a cherry colored lip gloss. I felt better about how I looked; not sure why I cared to fix my appearance in the first place. Now, why was I frontin'? I didn't want that nigga seeing me looking a hot mess.

As I made my way back out to the front of the coffee shop, I took shorter steps when I saw him standing at the counter. Cocoa had him in a conversation that he didn't seem interested in. She was being her usual thot self----overly sexy.

As I took in his attire, I understood fully why he was called, Gucci

Boss. This nigga was dripping in Gucci! He wore a pair of black Gucci jeans, a white Gucci belt, and a black Gucci sweater that sat nicely on his muscled frame. The only thing that wasn't Gucci was his sneakers. They were all white Jordan's.

Cocoa's eyes followed me as I came up behind him. Seeing her eyes look behind him, caused him to turn in my direction. Damn! He looked even more handsome than earlier.

"Wassup, shawty?" He smiled at me which showed off a full, upper gold grill.

I don't remember seeing that earlier. "Hey," was the only thing that I managed to say as I stood to the side of him.

"You ready to bounce?" he asked me and stopped leaning on the counter.

I had no idea of how he planned to fix my mirror. I hadn't even bothered to ask. "How're you going to fix my mirror?" I asked as I looked at the clock on the wall. I really needed to pick up my mom.

"You can just follow me. I got a homeboy that owns a garage." He took my hand in his and lead me out of the shop. I didn't want to feel childish by pulling my hand away, so I allowed him to guide me out the shop even though I barely knew him.

"I can't, Jayceon. I have to pick up my mom at 5:00," I said as I pulled my hand from his grip, forgetting my manners. I turned to say goodbye to Cocoa who was looking at me and Jayceon as if she was mad. That bitch hated whenever someone else got any type of attention.

"Well, let's go get her then." He took hold of my hand again and led me outside to his Range Rover.

I pulled away again. "Look, maybe we should do this another time. I have to go get her, so I can't follow you to your friend's garage. We can do this some other day." I walked to my car and took my car keys out of my bag. Then I heard footsteps behind me.

"Yo, why you playing with a nigga's feelings? Look, I'll have my homeboy take your car over to the garage, and then we'll go get your moms. I don't mind droppin' you guys off at home," he said as he reached for my arm and turned me around. I looked at him trying to figure out what game he was playing? Why was he so willing to help me out?

"Look, wait here, aight." He turned away and briskly jogged to his Range. He opened one of his back doors and it seemed as if he was talking to someone. Next thing I knew, two guys came out the back seat. They were both dressed in all black with hoodies drawn over their heads. As they approached me, I looked at their faces, then quickly looked away. I definitely wouldn't want to be alone with these two at any time. These niggas looked straight up scary! I was rendered speechless as Jayceon took my keys out of my hand.

"Shauntel, these are my boys, Maliq and Trevor." Jayceon gave a quick introduction of his friends. "Yo, take her car over to Vicks Chop Shop. He's expecting it."

Did this nigga just give my car keys over to somebody I didn't even know? He must be crazy! "Ummm, excuse you. I barely know you, and I don't know these fools. Nobody's leaving with my car," I said as I snatched my shit back from his friend who looked shocked at my boldness.

"Man, calm down. Ain't nobody tryna' steal no Toyota." Jayceon snatched the keys back and returned them to his friend. The two guys walked towards my car.

I turned and cut my eyes at Jayceon. "Now how in the hell am I gonna' get my car back?" I asked in a whining voice. *This is crazy! How did I allow a stranger to hand my car over to people I knew even less than him!*

"Let me worry about all that. C'mon, let's go get your moms." For what seemed liked the hundredth time, Jayceon took my hand and led me to his Range. He came over to the passenger side and actually opened the door for me, which surprised me.

When I peeped the interior as I hopped in, I began to think that Jayceon had some sort of complex. There was Gucci printed everywhere----the seats, the dashboard, the doors. *This nigga is out his damn mind.* As he took his seat behind the steering wheel, I turned and gave him my 'what the fuck' expression.

His top grill gleamed as he laughed. "What? A nigga can't like somethin' . . . A LOT!" he said as he started his vehicle. "Where we gonna' get your moms at?"

Hearing his question brought me back to reality. I cleared my throat before answering his question. "Piedmont Hospital," I said. I didn't bother to look at him, but I felt his eyes on me as I told him where we were headed. He asked nothing more as we pulled out of the parking lot.

"So, tell me about yourself, besides the fact that you can't drive for shit."

Was he really taking it there again, knowing damn well he broke the red light, I thought as I rolled my eyes. "Well, I attend Spelman

13

College, I'm nineteen, and I'm majoring in education studies. I'm an only child to my now deceased father, and a mother who is battling breast cancer." The last part of my introduction was said almost in a whisper and very quickly. I was hoping Jayceon wasn't able to catch everything that I said. The last thing I wanted was for him, or anyone for that matter, to feel sorry for me.

"My bad, shawty. I'm really sorry to hear about your moms. I really am."

I kept my eyes on the road and didn't look at him as he spoke. He sounded sincere enough. I didn't really like discussing my mom's health anyway. It was a sensitive topic for me.

"So, where yo' man at? He's supposed to be helping you hold shit down; like driving you to work and all that." Jayceon looked over at me slightly.

"Jayceon, I barely get five hours of sleep at night. I'm juggling college, a part-time job and taking care of my mother. When the hell am I going to find time to date?" I asked and chuckled slightly.

I couldn't even remember the last time somebody even asked me out. Besides, I was a virgin. Yup! My cherry had never been popped, and I had planned to keep it that way, too. These men out here play too much. I hear stories the college girls tell, and I can do without all that added stress from a nigga.

On top of all that, I was so busy most times. And before my dad passed away, he was so damn strict that I was never really allowed to go out much. My father used to chaperone me damn near everywhere. Being an only child was no fun half the time.

"So, you mean to tell me that you don't have a nigga in yo' life?" He looked at me incredulously as if he'd never heard anything like that before.

I shook my head.

"Hmmm, I bet you like those sensitive ass niggas that wear pink and are in touch with their feelings and all that bullshit." He chuckled at his own words.

I don't see anything wrong with wanting a man to treat you right. I saw how my father took good care of my mother, while making an honest living and providing for his family, and that's exactly what I wanted. I refused to settle for less. "So, what's wrong with wanting a sensitive brother?" I said as I looked out the window. I would put all my money on the idea that Jayceon couldn't give two shits about a woman and her feelings. To me, he looked like a man who cared very little.

"And what's your story, Gucci Boss!" I exclaimed, stressing his nickname, and smiling a little as I saw his expression change to a humorous one.

"I run the 'A'. End of mothafuckin' story," he said as he turned into the hospital's parking lot.

I wasn't in the mood to press him more for an autobiography of his life, so I let it slide. Besides, after I get my car fixed, it's not like I'll be seeing him again anyway.

He parked a couple feet away from the main entrance. I was about to let him know that I would be back in a few minutes when I saw him hop out the Range. I looked on as he made his way over to my side of the door and opened it. He waited for me to get out.

"You don't have to walk up with me to get her. I'll be OK," I said as I took his hand and let him help me out the van.

"Man, be quiet with all that noise and let's go get your moms." He took my hand and led me to the entrance.

What is it with him and holding hands? I thought. He definitely didn't seem like the holding hands type of nigga.

We took the elevator. As we stood in an uncomfortable silence, I felt Jayceon's eyes on me. *What is his problem?* I knew I wasn't his type. I see what street niggas are into; those ride-or-die, big booty, loud mouth, trap queen type bitches. I didn't fall into any of those categories. I couldn't deny that he was fine. I also couldn't deny that he was all wrong for me and would probably bring me nothing but trouble!

As the elevator came to a stop on the third floor where my mom's room was, I took off in a brisk walk and left Jayceon behind. Upon entering the room, I was pleasantly surprised to see that my mother was sitting up in bed and watching television. She smiled when she saw me.

"Shaunie, baby. You here to take me home?" my mother asked with a gleam in her eyes that I hadn't seen in a while.

I walked over to her, gave her a quick hug, and kissed her cheek. "Yeah, we're going home." I started getting her things together.

I looked at my mother and saw that she was staring at the doorway. When I turned around to see what she was looking at, I saw Jayceon walking into the room. *Shit! I swear, I almost forgot about him.*

"Uuummm . . . Mom, this is Jayceon. He ran into my car this morning after I left here. He took my car to get the mirror fixed, so he's going to give us a ride home, OK?" I said, knowing that I'd have to explain his presence to my mother.

"You got in an accident baby? Are you OK?" The worried look on her face caused my heart to ache. The last thing I wanted was to add any more stress on her. I rushed over to her and sat on the bed.

"Mom, it's o----". Before I could finish my sentence Jayceon interrupted.

"Nah, it was totally my fault ma'am. I wasn't paying attention and ran the red light. I'm sorry, I didn't get your name," Jayceon said as he held his hand out in a gesture of greeting towards my mother.

I looked at him in obvious shock. *Since when did he turn into a college professor and shit! Talking all proper and what not.* Not to mention that he finally admitted that he was in the wrong and caused our accident.

"My name is Jasmine Harris." My mother and Jayceon shook hands, and she gave him a weak smile.

"Look, I'll be right out here waiting for you guys. Let me give you your privacy, Mrs. Harris." Those were his parting words as he stepped out the room.

I got off the bed and continued the task of gathering her stuff so we could leave. I felt her eyes follow me all over the room, but I refused to meet her gaze.

"Mmmm. Well, he's handsome," I heard my mother say as I walked towards her to help her out of bed. I took the scarf out her knapsack and began covering her head, which had only a few strands of hair remaining due to Chemo.

"Is he? I hadn't noticed," I replied, lying through my teeth. Stevie Wonder could tell he was fine. I placed the scarf on her head, picked up her bag, and placed her in the wheel chair that had been sitting in the corner of the room.

As I wheeled her through the door, Jayceon came forward. He gently moved my hands. Without saying a word, he was letting me know that he would take my mom downstairs for me. I went to the nurses' station and let them know that I was leaving with her.

I met Jayceon and my mom by the elevator. As the doors opened, I waited for him to put her in before I entered. We stood side by side with my mom in her chair to the front of us. I was biting the inside of my lower lip as the elevator made its descent; his presence had my nerves on edge. I felt like a teenager who had a crush on the star football player.

I saw Jayceon take his hand off the handle of the chair. Before I knew what was happening, he reached for my hand. He entwined his fingers with mine and brushed his thumb back and forth over my fingers. My breath got caught in my throat at the wonderful sensation that coursed through my body. I instantly felt my body reacting; my nipples hardened and my pussy started to throb slightly. Feeling guilty because my mother was with us, I attempted to pull my hand out of his reach, but he held on tightly and didn't allow me to break free. I stole a quick glance at him, but he kept his head straight.

Finally, the elevator stopped, and the door opened. He removed his hand from mine and wheeled my mother through the exit towards his car. We both helped her out the chair and placed her in the back

18

seat. I took the wheel chair inside, then got in the Range.

"Where you live, shawty?" Jayceon asked as he looked at me and put the key in the ignition. I gave him directions and we headed to my home.

CHAPTER 3

I put my mother in bed after getting home safely. Jayceon waited for me on our porch to let me know the status of my car. As I walked outside to meet him, he stood.

"Look, your car won't be fixed 'till maybe tomorrow afternoon, aight?"

I stared at him incredulously. *How can it take a whole day to fix a damn mirror?*

"Are you serious right now Jayceon? How am I going to get to school in the morning? And what kind of mechanic can't even fix a mirror right away? It's not like the car has a dent or something!" *I didn't mean to be rude. After all, he'd been very nice to my mother.*

As I was about to apologize for being thoughtless, his phone rang. He took his phone out his pants pocket. As soon as he looked at the screen, he blew air as if he was annoyed. "What!" he exclaimed as he answered the phone.

I heard the echo of a female's voice from the other end, and from the tone of her voice, she was pissed! To say that I wasn't feeling some type of way about him talking to a female in my presence would be a lie. I bet that was his girlfriend who probably looked like Amber Rose,

Buffie the Body, or something like that.

"Man, go ahead with all that bullshit you throwin' at me right now."

I stood in silence as he ended the call abruptly. Whoever she was, she wasn't done talking before he'd hung up on her.

"Look, I'll swing by in the morning and take you to class. What time you need to be there?" he asked. He still looked irritated from his call. I saw his jaw tick a couple of times as if he was giving his best effort to control his anger.

"Jayceon, you just can't keep taking me everywhere. I need my car back." I huffed a sigh and folded my arms as I looked at him.

"And you'll get your car back. Chill out, aight. What time should I come get you?"

I wasn't used to anyone catering to my needs. I hesitated for a few seconds before telling him that I had to be at class at 8:00.

"I'll be here at 7:30, Be ready, aight? Don't have a nigga waiting and shit. Look, I got something I have to take care of." He squeezed my arm gently as he turned to leave. He jumped in his vehicle and drove off.

If Jayceon didn't make sure that I got my car back tomorrow, I was going to be mad as hell, I thought as I walked back inside to see about my mother.

*****

At exactly 7:30 the next morning, there was a knock on my front door. I'd been dressed and waiting ten minutes before. I assisted my mom with her hygiene before I left as always. I made sure that she had a bath and was fed. Our neighbor would come at about noon to stay with her until I got home.

I stood in the mirror and scanned my appearance; I wore a black and white tie-dyed maxi dress with a sleeveless denim jacket and a pair of black, strapped sandals. My hair was down. I had straightened it earlier. I quickly walked to the front door and opened it just as Jayceon was about to knock one more time. *Well damn!* I thought as I took all of him in.

He wore white Levi's, a black V-neck t-shirt with Gucci color strips on the sides, and a pair of Jordan's as usual. He took his Gucci shades off and smiled at me. "You ready Shaunie?" he said as his eyes roamed over me with a look of appreciation.

"Let me tell my mom that I'm leaving, OK." I said, as I went to my mom's room. She was sitting in bed with her scarf on, looking at some random movie on Netflix.

"Mom, I'm about to leave, OK. Jayceon's taking me to class. Call me if you need anything. Ms. Johnson will be over in a couple of hours." I smiled and kissed her slender face. During the last couple of months, she'd grown so frail from the cancer and the treatments.

"You be careful with that guy. He's handsome and all, but you know what they say, baby—all that glitters ain't gold!" My mother gave me a look of warning.

What! My mother was tripping. Nothing is going to happen between me and Jayceon. All I wanted was my car back, then he could go back to running the "A". That's not my business.

"Mom, don't be silly. All he's doing is helping me out with my car. That's it. Besides, I'm pretty sure I'm not his type anyway," I said while slightly shaking my head. My mother let out a sigh, and I turned to her.

"You're such a naïve little girl. I blame your father for always trying to hide you from the world," she said softly.

She'd always told me that I had no idea of how beautiful I was, and that if a man was interested in me, I wouldn't have a clue.

"Stop, OK. I love you. See you later." I kissed her and left the room to meet Jayceon who was sitting as he waited on me.

He stood up when he saw me. I grabbed my bag from the sofa that he'd been was sitting. I then took my backpack off my shoulder so he could hold it for me. He took my hand and led me to the front door.

"C'mon, let's go get you educated. Your moms got a nurse that comes to see about her?" he asked as he waited on me to lock the front door.

"No, I can't afford that right now. But my next-door neighbor comes over to stay with her until I get home."

Jayceon looked as if he didn't find that to be a good idea, but he didn't say anything. As he and I walked towards the street, I was expecting to see his Range Rover parked out front. Instead, I saw a custom designed Gucci Maybach.

My steps came to a halt as I stared in disbelief. "What in the hell!"

"Now this baby right herrre is the real reason they call me Gucci Boss," he said as he spread his hands out wide and smiled at his car.

I looked at his excited face, and couldn't help the smile that came across my lips as I looked at Jayceon. Talk about a kid in a candy store. Jayceon was obviously a proud poppa. I was never one to be into the flashy type of lifestyle, so I wasn't really fazed much.

He held the door open for me as I hopped in, then handed me my backpack after he was sitting behind the wheel,

"What's up with my car Jayceon? I can't go another day without it," I said to him as he drove away from my street.

I lived about fifteen minutes away from Spelman, so we'd be there soon.

"You'll get it back today, Shaunie. Relax. I got you."

I don't really know how I felt about him calling me by my nickname. Only my parents called me that, but I decided to let it slide. Maybe Cocoa was right? Maybe I am stuck up.

"Let me play this song for you real quick," he said putting the radio on. The sound of Fetty Wap quickly filled the inside of the car:

"Baby, won't you come my wayyyyy.

Got something I want to sayyyyy" . . .

Jayceon sang along with the song as he reached for my hand.

He told me that I couldn't drive for shit, but he couldn't sing for shit. He *is a horrible singer*, I thought to myself as he crooned along with the song. But I'll be damned if I wasn't flattered. *This shit right here has never happened to me in my life. I got this street nigga who was supposed to be all hard and shit, trying his best to sing me a song before dropping me off to college. Is this what dreams are made of?*

On our way, I learned a few things about Jayceon. He was a

twenty-three-year-old high school dropout. His father was shot in front of him when he was sixteen years old. Being the oldest of three kids, one sister and one brother, he took on the responsibility of being the bread-winner of his family. So, he started running the streets, and pretty soon he was practically running his own empire.

The reason his father was killed was because of a drug deal gone sour. He stole some bricks from his connect, and the connect had no problem smoking him. The stolen bricks were found by his then sixteen-year-old son, Jayceon, who was hidden in the trunk of his father's Mercedes Benz. Jayceon was already known in the streets, so it wasn't hard for him to hook up with the local dope boys to sell his product. And I guess, the rest is history as they say. He'd been running shit in the ATL ever since.

The looks that we got as he dropped me off, were a little embarrassing. Everyone's eyes were glued to the Gucci Maybach. I asked him if he would be bringing my car to school later.

"Nah, I'll take you to get it. What time you get out?" he asked as he slowly licked his full lips and looked at me seductively. It was as if he was trying tease me, and it worked. I replied that I'll be there until three, and he responded by letting me know that he'd be back to get me. As I started opening the door, he softly grabbed my upper arm.

"Have a good day. Aight, shawty?"

Before I knew what was about to happen, he leaned in and gently kissed my lips. His lips were so soft just as I thought they'd be. I loved the way they felt on mine, and they tasted like chocolate. Maybe he'd had a cup of hot chocolate before he came to get me? I felt his breathe on my face as he pulled away slowly, leaving me breathless and wanting more. My clit was pulsing like crazy in my panties, and I clamped my thighs together as if that would somehow help.

"O----OK, bye," I stuttered and felt a little foolish about how he'd made me feel.

As I got out and headed up the steps, a girl who'd never spoken to me before said, "Damn girl, how you know Gucci Boss?"

If she wanted a reply from me, that was her problem. I kept it moving and went to class with a slight smile on my face.

CHAPTER 4

My day at school was a total waste. My concentration was on zero. Every chance I got, my fingers were on my lips, reminiscing about the way Jayceon's full lips felt pressed against mine.

Previous to that, I'd only been kissed one other time. It was when I was thirteen and I played a game of spin the bottle at a birthday party. The boy's name was Tevin. His kiss was rough compared to Jayceon's. He stuck his tongue harshly into my mouth, which was a complete turn off.

As my day at school was coming to an end, I started feeling butterflies in my stomach at the thought of seeing Jayceon again.

On my way towards the front exit, I heard someone call out to me. "Hey, Shauntel."

I turned around after I heard my name. I was greeted by the face of a substitute teacher, Mr. Evans, who was only a few years older than I was. We had become quite acquainted over the past few months that he'd worked here. He wasn't a bad looking guy. He favored Morris Chestnut; same complexion, baldheaded, goatee, and a toned body.

"You done for the day?" he questioned as he walked with me towards the exit.

Mr. Evans was studying law and hoped to become a lawyer. He landed the role of substitute because the English teacher was on maternity leave. He told me that his father was a well-known police officer in Atlanta who was hoping that his only son would follow in his footsteps. Chase, however, said he didn't want any part of being in the police service.

"Hey, Mr. Evans. Yeah, I'm about to leave."

I heard him take a sharp inhale of air. He hated that I called him Mr. Evans; said it made him feel old.

"I'm sorry, Chase. Yes, I'm done for the day," I said correcting his name and smiling as I did so.

"If my memory serves me correctly, you've got a birthday coming up, right?"

Shit! I completely forgot that my twentieth birthday was just couple weeks away.

"Thanks for reminding me. I almost forgot about that," I said shaking my head. My life was in such disarray that I almost forgot I was about to turn twenty.

"Well, you know Mrs. Chambers will be back soon; meaning that I'll be gone soon. So, maybe we could celebrate both things in one?"

I didn't quite get what he was saying. "Huh, what'chu mean?" Was he asking me out? Remember when my mother said I was naïve? That shit was no joke. If a guy was interested in me, I was usually the last one to figure it out.

"Well . . . it's your birthday, and I'll be leaving soon to finish my law degree. So, let's kill two birds with one stone. What you think?"

Even though he wasn't a legit teacher at the college, I was skeptical on whether or not that would be a good idea. This was a small world. I could only imagine the gossip if someone were to see me and him out together.

"Can you give me some time to think about it?" I asked as we approached the doorway, even though I already knew that I was going to say no.

"Sure, why not. Let me give you my number in case you change your mind." He took my phone from my hand and he logged his number in. As we made our way down the steps, he handed my phone back to me. "I'll see you around. Aight, Shauntel?" He smiled at me. I smiled back and waved goodbye.

As I continued walking, I saw Jayceon standing on the passenger side of his Range Rover. He was looking at me as I made my way towards him. He had a strange expression on his face. As I approached, he opened the door for me. but didn't say anything. Is he mad or something, I thought as I climbed in.

As he got in and closed the door, he turned to me. "Who that is?" he asked, confusing me a bit with his question.

"Who are you talking about?" I asked and looked back at him with a confused look on my face.

"Who's the homeboy that was giving you back your phone, man?"

What in the hell. Jayceon must be crazy. I don't know why he thinks that he could question me about who I'm talking to. "That's just a sub. Why you care?" I asked as he started the car and pulled off. I was checking out the way his muscles hugged his t-shirt. He probably worked out every day to get a physique like that.

"Don't get homeboy fucked up!"

I laughed a little but didn't mean to. I couldn't help it. I've known Jayceon for all of two days, and he thinks that he can tell me who I can and can't talk to?

"I don't know why you're laughing when I'm dead ass serious. Just in case you haven't noticed, I'm feeling the fuck outta' you. Ever since you came out of your car, and I saw how sexy you were, I knew you had to be mine. And I plan on doing whatever I need to do to make sure that you are. Plus, I know that pussy ain't never been touched. I'm gon' make you mine. Just watch and see."

His words definitely left me in disbelief. Here I was thinking all along that I wasn't his type when I actually was. And how the fuck did he know that I was a virgin? Was he some kind of virgin whisperer or something?

"So, you like me? Why do you like me?" I surely wanted to hear this. I looked at him with an eager expression.

When I looked in the mirror, I didn't see the type of woman that Jayceon seemed like he'd be interested in. But maybe I was underestimating myself?

"Why wouldn't I like you? You sexy as fuck, you smart, and maybe you could get a nigga to change his ways eventually and get out these streets. I like that you low-key; not what I'm used to with these thirsty bitches tryna get at me for my stacks. These hoes out here be doin' too much."

I listened attentively as he spoke and was surprised out my damn mind. Who would've thought that he'd be interested in little old me? I for sure didn't.

"So, let's kick it. I know you ain't never had a street nigga. I respect that you want to handle your responsibilities on your own and all that, but even Superman needs a day off. Just relax and let me take care of your every need like a real man supposed to. The first thing we're going to do is get a nurse to take care of your moms when you ain't around. Your moms needs proper care. That ain't no joke."

My mind was a whirlwind of thoughts. My daddy will do flips in his grave if I got involved with somebody like Jayceon. I knew absolutely nothing about his type of lifestyle, and I for damn sure wasn't used to being taken care of. I looked over at him as he kept his eye on the road. We were on our way to get my car. *This was something that I have to think about before I got in way over my head*, I thought to myself.

"I don't know, Jayceon. I mean, you seem nice and all, but I'm not used to being around the type of lifestyle that you're into. Plus, I'm really not used to anyone handling my responsibilities but me," I said as I innocently twisted my hands in my lap.

He pulled up to the car shop and brought the Range to a stop. He turned in his seat and took my hands in his. "Look at me, Shauntel."

I did what he said and looked at him shyly. He took my chin in his hand, our eyes made contact.

"My lifestyle ain't got shit to do with you. I'm gon' respect that you don't wanna fuck with what I do, but I'll be damned if I let you slip through my fingers because I run these mothafuckin' streets. I'm feeling you way too much, shawty. Just give a nigga a chance to show you how much, aight?"

I started biting on my lower lip and thinking about what he'd said. I saw his gaze turn to the way that I bit my lip.

"I love it when you do that," he said hoarsely and dipped his head toward mine.

He slowly took my lower lip between his lips, sucked on it gently, and nibbled on it once, then again. When his mouth finally made full contact with mine, I almost lost my mind. He was an expert in kissing; the way he let his tongue snake into my mouth and then collide with mine; the way he used the tip of his tongue to trace the outline of my top, then bottom lip; the way he sucked gently, then a bit more aggressively on my lower lip. I couldn't help the moan that escaped me when he finally pulled away.

"I bet that pussy wet for a nigga, huh?"

Suddenly, feeling shy and even embarrassed, I tilted my head at what he'd said because he was right. My pussy was dripping for him.

"C'mon, let's go get your car," he said as he opened the door and hopped out his whip.

I reached for the handle and opened my door. When I got out, my legs felt like Jell-O. If I'd known that Jayceon was going to turn my life into a twisted, emotional wreck, I would've fixed my goddamn mirror myself!

CHAPTER 5

My birthday was slowly approaching. It'd been a week and a half since Jayceon literally crashed into my life. There hadn't been a day that he wasn't in contact with me. He made it his business to either take me to class, pick me up from class, take me to my job, or pick me up from my job, whether I wanted his ass to or not! When my mom had another chemotherapy appointment, he made sure that he was present; holding my hand as we waited. He was still insisting that I get a home care provider for her. But I was still reluctant to giving in; not because I didn't want to, but because I couldn't afford such an exorbitant expense.

I was trying my best to not give into his advances towards me. Lord knows my daddy would come into my dreams to hit me upside my head if I got involved with Jayceon. So, I kept him at arm's length. But damn, if that man wasn't so fine, it would've been easier.

On days when I didn't see him because he had to be in the streets, he made sure to keep in touch via text or call. Today was one of those days. He said that he had a shipment coming in that he needed to be there to oversee. Even though I wasn't OK with what he did, I was OK with the fact that he'd kept his word and the street aspect of his life to himself so far. I knew a little, but not very much about his operations.

As I was leaving for class to go to work, I felt someone tap me on my shoulder. When I turned around, I saw that it was Mr. Evans.

"Hey Mr. Ev—" I stopped mid-sentence because I remembered that he didn't liked to be called that.

"Hey, Chase, how you been?" I smiled at him.

"Today is my last day here, you know? I haven't heard from you since we last talked. Did you give what we spoke about any thought?"

I had honestly forgotten about Chase's proposal to take me out. I'd been so caught up with Jayceon that I'd completely forgotten. That didn't matter though because I didn't think it would've been a good idea anyway.

"I'm sorry, Chase. It's been a crazy week for me. I don't think I'll be able to go celebrate with you. I'm sorry. But I am supposed to be going to that new club that opened up the other day."

About two days ago, Jayceon mentioned that he would take me to his friend's club on the night of my birthday. I wasn't certain if I should go because I was thinking about my mom. But he told me that he'd hire a nurse for that night only.

"Oh, you mean the BHive?" he asked.

"Yeah, that's the one," I said as I shook my index finger at him.

"Well, I guess I'll see you there. That's actually where I had in mind for us to go kick it anyway." He smiled sweetly.

Chase was a very good-looking guy. I wondered a few times about if he had a girlfriend, but quickly brushed it off. We talked for a few more minutes then said our good-byes. I then headed to work.

*****

It was a slow day at the coffee shop, so Cocoa and I decided to close a few minutes early. As we cleaned and chatted about the last episode of the TV show, "Power", my phone began ringing. I grabbed it from my pocket knowing that it would be Jayceon checking on me. As I watched the screen, I saw an unknown number. That's odd; nobody ever called me unknown.

"Hello?" I said as I picked up some empty coffee cups off a table and walked towards the trash.

"Bitch, why the fuck do you keep calling and texting my man, Gucci?" an unfamiliar female voice demanded.

I stopped mid-stride, had to pull the phone away from my ear, and check the screen again. I had no idea who homegirl was, but she needed to check her attitude. "Excuse you? Who is this?" I was pretty sure whoever this was had dialed the wrong number.

"This is his BM. And who are you?"

Even though I wasn't your regular street chick, I knew what BM stood for. The cups I'd been holding fell to the floor. Cocoa stopped what she was doing and came over to me.

"What the fuck did you just say?" I rarely cursed, but when I did, it was called for. I now had Cocoa's full attention as she stood before me.

The female on the other end chuckled at my response. "Gucci always be playing with you hoes feelings. I'm Nae Nae. Welcome to the family you dumb bitch!" she said and then hung up.

I took my cell away from my ear and looked at it in total disbelief. *His baby momma! What in the hell. Did this fool forget to mention that he had a child with someone?*

"Girl, what the hell? Are you aight?" Cocoa questioned me as she bent to pick up the cups that had fallen out of my hand.

"You won't believe what that call was about. Some trick said she's Jayceon's baby momma." Cocoa looked at me and then started laughing.

"Girl, I know yo' ass ain't used to niggas like Gucci, but you have more than just that one phone call you gon' have to deal with. Men like Gucci come with all different types of baggage and problems. Trust me. Young B have me cussin' out bitches every Monday morning. You got more coming your way, girl." Cocoa threw the cups in the trash.

More to come my way! I'll be damned if Jayceon thought he'd have his flavors of the week calling my phone, cursin' me out!

"Did you know he had a baby with someone?" I asked even though I felt ashamed that I had to ask Cocoa a question that I should know myself.

Cocoa laughed. "Girl, let me tell yo' ass sumthin'. Don't ever assume these niggas are just gon' share shit with yo' ass. What you wanna know, you either ask, or snoop the fuck out they ass. So, I suggest your lil' boujee self get to questioning Gucci's ass."

With those final words, she walked to the kitchen and left me with my thoughts. Jayceon had told me that he would swing by my house after he was done with his connect. *When he comes over to my place, I'm gonna' do exactly what Cocoa said----ask him. Why would he not answer me?*

CHAPTER 6

"*M*om, do you mind if I go out for my birthday?" I was checking on my mom as I always did after I arrived home from work. Jayceon had texted me saying that he would be over in about twenty minutes. I was patiently waiting on him.

"Of course not, Shaunie. You don't even have to ask," she replied. She patted my hand affectionately as I adjusted the covers around her body.

"Do you think you'll be alright if a nurse takes care of you that evening? 'Cause if you're not, I won't go anywhere." I stood and waited for a reply. If my mother wasn't comfortable being with a stranger then, I wouldn't be going anywhere that night.

"Sure, baby, you deserve to have some fun." Where you going to get a nurse though?" she asked as she slightly creased her forehead.

"You let me worry about that. Have a good night, OK." I kissed her cheek, and her eyes closed. I then walked away and prepared for Jayceon's arrival.

After taking a quick bath, I slipped into a pair of cotton shorts and a thin strap top. I put my hair in a messy bun then sat in the living room and watched TV. I wasn't paying attention to what was on TV because my mind was buzzing as I anxiously waited on Jayceon. I wasn't the type of female that would start drama, but I wanted to know if what Nae Nae had said was true.

There was a soft knock on the front door. I got up quickly and ran to answer the door. I was greeted with a bear hug after I let Jayceon in.

"Wassup, Shaunie?" He kissed my lips and tugged so aggressively at my lower lip that it hurt.

I was learning how to respond to his advances without being too timid. I opened my mouth and allowed his tongue access. Our tongues twirled and entwined, and I groaned softly. At that moment, I'd forgotten that I should be questioning his ass.

I pulled away from his embrace, then took his hand and led him inside. We walked hand in hand to the sofa and sat down.

"You miss me today bae?" he asked as he rubbed his hand on my upper thighs, which caused my hairs to raise. I kept reminding myself not to lose focus.

"Yeah, I did. By the way, I got a strange call today."

He looked at me with his head cocked to one side. Then he took off his snapback. That's when I noticed that he wasn't rocking anything Gucci; just a plain white tee that hugged his muscular body, a black pair of Tru Religion jeans, and of course, those damn Jordan's.

"Oh yeah? From who?"

"Nae Nae. That name sound familiar to you?" I took a mental picture of the way his facial expression changed with the mention of her name. I had hit him with a curve ball.

"Oh, word! What she want?"

Uh uh. Is Jayceon for real right now! All this fool can say is, "What she want"? I ought to get up and punch him in his damn throat!

"Jay, why you ain't never tell me you had a baby with somebody! Talking 'bout, 'what she want.' How can you keep that from me?" I pushed his roaming hand from off my thigh.

"Man, you ain't never ask if I have a seed."

Right then and there, Cocoa's words came back to haunt me. How stupid of me! I assumed that he'd be happy to let me know that he has a mini-me running around.

"Really, Jay? I had to ask if you have a child." I narrowed my eyes at him and wanted nothing more than to hit him upside his big head.

"Aight, Shauntel. Damn. Yes, I do have a son, he's two. His name is Jaden. My bad, aight?"

He said that shit like it was no big deal; like I was being a nag for wanting to know the truth. He tried to continue rubbing on my thigh, but I swatted his hand away.

"When were you planning on telling me, Jay?" Irritation showed on his face. I decided that maybe I was asking too much and that I should forget it so that he wouldn't get mad at me.

"Man, I came over here to spend some time with yo' ass, and this is the thanks I get. You drillin' me about a question you never even bothered to ask!" Jayceon jumped out his seat and stood before me with his hand in my face.

When I started inquiring about Nae Nae, it was certainly not my intention to make him mad. I started questioning myself and the idea that I was wrong to ask him about Nae Nae. So, I decided to apologize.

"Look, Jay. Don't be mad at me. I didn't mean anything by it. It's just that the last thing I expected when I answered my phone was someone saying that you and her have a baby together." I didn't want him to be angry, so I reached for his hand.

"Man, Nae Nae always on some shit. That's why me and her can't ever see eye to eye. You never have to worry about her coming between us. That's my word. Forget all that. I missed you. Come here."

When Jayceon touched me and planted his lips on mine, all was to be forgotten. I was so inexperienced with men that I never thought to ask him how it was possible that his baby momma had gotten my number in the first place if they didn't get along like he said.

But the way his mouth was working against mine was magic. I didn't even care!

CHAPTER 7

*I*t was the day before my birthday, and I was excited as I worked my last hour before closing time at the coffee shop. My mood was on high, and I kept looking at the clock on the wall in anticipation of Jayceon picking me up from work. We were going to the mall so that we could shop for clothes for our night at the club tomorrow.

The whole incident with his baby momma, Nae Nae had been pushed to the back of my mind. I was reassured by Jayceon that he put her in check and that she definitely wouldn't call me anymore. Hearing that was a relief.

"Oooh, who's that cutie that just came in the shop? Damn girl, that nigga can get the business from me any damn time."

I rolled my eyes as I listened to Cocoa go off. She was always eye raping these customers. I turned to see who her latest victim was, and my eyes came in contact with a pair of familiar ones.

"Chase! What are you doing here?" I was shocked. This was the first time he'd come into the shop.

"Well, I was driving by and suddenly got a craving for a cup of Cappuccino."

Chase has the most even set of pearly white teeth that I've ever seen in my life, I thought as he smiled at me. "Well, you've certainly come to the right place." I started making his order. He stood to the side and never took his eyes off me.

"Come sit and have a cup with me. I'm sure you can use a break?"

I was about to thank him and decline the offer, but was interrupted when big-mouthed bitch, Cocoa, jumped into our conversation.

"Go 'head, girl. I'll cover for you. Besides, it ain't that busy. Take a break." She winked at me and pushed me away from the register.

Not having much of a choice, I walked over to an empty table and sat with Chase.

"So, big day tomorrow, huh?" He took a sip of his coffee

"Yes, it is."

"Are you excited about turning the big 2-0?" Chase put his cup down and licked the foam from off his upper lip.

I realized that I was paying way too much attention to his full, thick lips, so I looked away and cleared my throat. "I guess so. Are you still hittin' up the club tomorrow night?" I asked him. This would actually be my first time partying at a club, and I was looking forward to it.

"I'm not sure. Are you still gonna' to be there?"

The way he looked at me when he asked that question caused me to shift uncomfortably in my seat. "My plans haven't changed. So, yes, I'll be there."

Chase held my gaze as he took a sip of his coffee. Even though I tried, I couldn't look away.

"Who are you going with?"

Had Chase and I not been so engrossed in our conversation, we would've realized that we were no longer alone.

"She's going with me, my nigga. Wassup?"

Hearing Jayceon's voice surprised me so much that I almost fell out my damn chair. I swung my head around.

"He----hey, Jay. I didn't see you come in."

I turned my attention to Cocoa with fire in my eyes. She could've at least given me warning that Jayceon was here. The look I received from Jayceon was enough to let me know that he wasn't happy seeing me chatting it up with Chase. Chase on the other hand, seemed unconcerned. He continued drinking his coffee as he took in Jayceon's Gucci attire, which left him with an amused look on his face.

"Man, who's this fuck boy you sittin' here kickin' it with?" Jayceon scanned Chase as if he was an insect.

The rude description that he gave of Chase was uncalled for, and his attitude was unnecessary. I stood up, folded my arms, and narrowed my eyes at Jayceon. "Jay, don't be rude."

"Nah, it's cool, Shauntel. It's time for me to go anyway." Chase got up. He took his time as he gathered his cup and wallet from the table. He took one last look at Jayceon and smiled. "Nice outfit by the way," he said as he nonchalantly walked toward the front door.

Why did he have to say that, I thought as I shook my head.

"Fuck you mean. This shit is worth more than a year of your salary, mothafucka." Jayceon took steps in Chase's direction as he spoke.

I quickly stood in his way and put my hands on his chest. I tried to defuse the situation, which I felt somewhat responsible for. "Jay, stop. OK. He's a substitute teacher at the college. He just came for a cup of coffee," I said in an attempt to convince him that Chase's visit was only a friendly one.

Jayceon looked at me with a scowl on his face. "Miss me with your lame ass explanation. I told yo' ass you gon' get homeboy fucked up. Don't think I didn't realize that's the same fool who walked out of school with you the other day. I'm waiting on your ass in the Range." Jayceon walked outside and hopped in his whip.

"You could've at least warned me that Jayceon was here, Cocoa," I said as I gathered my belongings and prepared to leave. Cocoa would be locking the shop on her own.

"Bitch, keep your eyes on your own goddamn affairs. That ain't my business, shit!"

I scrunched my nose at her before I turned to make my way outside to Jayceon's Range Rover. I opened the door and hopped inside. Jayceon didn't say two words to me as he drove to Lenox Square Mall.

*****

When you're not familiar with shopping for a night at the club, it can be exhausting. With Jayceon barely speaking to me, I had to figure out what I should wear on my own. We'd been to a total of six stores and I still hadn't chosen an outfit.

I let out a frustrated sigh, stopped dead in my tracks, and looked at Jayceon. "Look, this makes no sense. You're not speaking to me, and I have no idea what I should buy. Let's just go."

As I turned on my heel and looked for the nearest exit, I felt Jayceon grab my wrist. He turned me around, put his hand on my chin, and forced me to look at him.

"Even though I'm pissed the fuck off at you, we can't leave without getting you something to wear. Aight? Let's hit up the Fendi store." Jayceon took my hand and led me to the escalator.

Fendi! I can't afford to buy anything in that store. "Jayceon, I can't afford Fendi. Are you kidding me right now?" I pulled away from him like a stubborn child.

"Shaunie, do you seriously think I brought you to the mall so you can buy your own shit? Kinda' nigga you take me for?" Jayceon took my hand again and led me to the escalator.

I thought of possible ways that I could repay him because there was no way that I was going to let him buy me something as expensive as Fendi and not repay him.

We entered the store and walked around. Looking at the price tags. I was baffled by how much the items cost! *Who was shopping at this store? Oprah!*

"Jayceon, these prices are way too high. Let's go," I whispered harshly in his ear.

Without paying attention to what I'd said, Jayceon walked over to a rack that had a black jumpsuit on it. He picked it up, held it to me, and smiled. His grill shined. "Yo, this is gon' look good on that sexy body of yours. Go try this shit on, shawty."

I took the barely-there material from his hand, held it up, and inspected it. Jayceon couldn't expect me to leave my house looking like a stripper! "Jayceon, you done lost your mind. I can't wear this!" I shoved the jumpsuit back in his hand. I was appalled that he would think that I should wear something like that.

"Man, c'mon." Jayceon grabbed me by my hand and led me towards the changing room. He opened the door, and damn near shoved me in.

I held the fabric and analyzed it. I began stripping out of my work t-shirt and skinny jeans, then slipped on the jumpsuit one leg at a time. I looked in the mirror and inspected myself. The black jumpsuit was short. It stopped mid-way on my thighs. As I spun around and examined myself, I saw that it had a sweetheart cut and was scooped extremely low in the back. I'd be very much exposed.

"Aye, yo'. Hurry up, Shaunie. A nigga don't have all day." Jayceon tapped on the door softly.

I opened it and stood before him. He smiled, approvingly. "You sexy as fuck, ma," he said as he walked around me. "We definitely gettin' you this."

I was about to oppose, but I quickly changed my mind. Jayceon finally seemed like he'd forgotten about the whole Chase incident, and I refused to give him another reason to be upset. So, I didn't protest as he led me to the register.

CHAPTER 8

*M*y birthday was officially here. I'd been in and out of hair and nail salons all day. Jayceon arranged for me to be pampered all day long. He even brought his little sister, Jazmine, along so she could get her hair and nails done also.

It was now time for us to head to the club. I stood in the full-length mirror in my room, and I swore that I was damn near unrecognizable. My hair had extensions and was now mid-way down my back. My face was made-up beautifully with false eyelashes included. I was also three inches taller; thanks to the spanking new Gucci heels that Jayceon had got me. I can't lie; I was rocking the hell out of my jumpsuit. Despite loving the way I looked, this style was something that I wasn't used to.

I took a deep breath and walked to my mother's room. The nurse that Jayceon hired had been there all day taking care of her needs. My mother was sitting in a chair, and when she laid her eyes on me, I saw a flicker of disapproval about my appearance. But she quickly masked it with a fake smile.

"Well, well, Shaunie. Don't we look all grown up?" She let her gaze take in all of me from my head to my three-inch heeled feet.

"Thanks, Mom. How are you feeling? If you need me for

anything, don't hesitate to call. OK?" I bent forward and gently kissed her forehead.

"You go and have fun. The nurse you paid is doing a good job so far. Just be careful."

Of course, I couldn't tell her that Jayceon paid for the nurse. She would've accused me of accepting charity.

As I was adjusting the pillows behind her back, I heard knocking at the door. Butterflies re-surfaced at the expectation of seeing Jayceon. I had no idea of what the night may hold, or what he planned to do with me. I knew how men thought though. I wasn't ready for Jayceon to sample my goodies yet. Just because he bought my outfit and saw to it that my hair and makeup were on point, didn't mean that he was going to get the business!

I walked to the door and opened it for a smiling Jayceon. And boy, did he look fine! He was wearing a pair of slim-fit Gucci khaki pants, a black t-shirt with the Gucci logo in the center, a black leather jacket with the Gucci colors around the collar, and a retro pair of all white Jordan's. He wore two gold chains that hung loosely around his neck; one had a Jesus pendant. His gold upper grill gleamed as he smiled.

"Happy birthday again, baby. All the niggas in the club gon' wish they were me tonight!" He swooped his head down to gain access to my mouth. He kissed me with a greed and hunger that I'd never experienced from him before. He groped and grabbed my ass as he forced his tongue into my mouth.

"C'mon, let's go, aight," he said as he pulled his mouth away.

I walked out the door following his lead. When I saw the stretch

Hummer limo parked out front, I almost pissed my drawers. "You love drawing attention to yourself, don't you?" I said as he opened the door for me.

"This is what I do. A nigga be flossin," Jayceon said as he opened the door for me. Upon entering the limo, I was greeted by an entourage of nothing but gangstas! I recognized two guys from the first day that I met Jayceon; Maliq and Trevor who took my car to the chop shop. They were well dressed, but still scary as hell. There were also two others; one redbone nigga and another with dreads.

"I got a surprise for you, shawty," Jayceon whispered in my ear and then sucked lightly on my earlobe.

The shivers I felt when his mouth connected on my sensitive skin had my knees were shaking. I thought, *it's a good thing that I'm already seated.* Jayceon pulled me closer to him as the limo drove off.

"Oh, yeah? What's that?" I couldn't stop staring into his brown eyes. I was officially hypnotized. Jayceon had me all in my feelings. I was sprung!

"You'll see. Don't worry."

Oblivious to the other people that were sharing the limo with us, Jayceon and I kissed passionately. I didn't care. I was on cloud nine.

I sat in the VIP lounge with my third glass of Hennessy in hand. We'd been at the club for a couple hours now, and it was packed. Jayceon's homeboy, who owned the club, was definitely going to make a mint tonight! The spectacle before me had me speechless. Jayceon and his friends were acting a damn fool; Drake's "Hotline Bling" played, and Jayceon and his friends sang every word!

You used to call me on my cell phone

Late night when you need my love

And I know when that hotline bling

That could only mean one thing

I didn't know whether to laugh or cry as I watched Jayceon imitate the exact dance moves that Drake did in his video as he drank Moet straight from the bottle. This nigga and his crew are as drunk as anyone could get, I thought as I watched them throw Moet on each other. Each had their own bottle in hand.

This Hennessy is no joke, I thought as I got up to use the bathroom.

After seeing me stand up, Jayceon staggered over to me. "Yo, where your sexy ass think you goin'?" His words were slurring something terrible as he spoke.

"I'll be right back, OK? Just gonna' use the bathroom real quick," I said in his ear as he held his hand possessively around my waist.

"Aight, hurry yourself up." He slapped me on my ass as I turned to walk in the direction of the bathroom.

After using the bathroom, I stepped out to wash my hands. I noticed two females enter. Always one to mind my own business, I paid them no mind as I dried my hands with paper towels and prepared to go back to Jayceon and his crew.

"Aye, bitch. You here with my man?"

Completely confused, I looked behind me to see who this chick was talking to.

"The fuck you looking behind you for? I'm talking to your slow ass!"

I took a good look at the female that stood before me. She could've passed for a way more ghetto and slutty version of the singer, Rihanna. She was tall and light skinned with hazel brown eyes. Her Brazilian bundles fell in a cascade of curls down to her ass. What made her different from Rihanna was that she had mad curves, thick thighs, and a huge ass. She wore a short, black faux leather halter dress.

"Excuse me? But I think you may have me mistaken for somebody else," I said as I made my way to the exit. When I attempted to pass *Ren* and *Stimpy,* they blocked my path. I looked at them and was beginning to get pissed off.

"Bitch! You here partying it up with my man Gucci. I know exactly who you are!" she said while pointing her neon colored stiletto nails in my face.

"Who the fuck are you?" After three glasses of Hennessey, I was feeling as if I could whoop both this trick and her friend's ho ass; never mind that I couldn't fight worth a damn!

"Nae Nae, bitch!"

Before I had time to respond, she grabbed my hair and pulled me forward. I was in so much shock that I didn't have time to defend myself. There were hands on just about every part of my body. Nae Nae and her little Minion were beating my ass!

I don't know when we ended up outside the bathroom door and into full view of the club. I was trying futilely to defend myself, but Nae Nae and her friend were simply too much. Nae Nae kept hitting me in my face, and her friend had a death grip on my hair. I was flailing my hands wildly in an attempt to get these two wild animals off my ass.

"Bitch, get the fuck off her!" I heard Jayceon's voice. I heard other voices, also; They were from the guys in Jayceon's crew as they pulled those primitive beasts off me.

"Jayceon, you always out in these damn streets with these mothafuckin' hoes. Why you always do me like that?" I regained my composure, fixed my hair, and stood upright as Jayceon came to my side; I adjusted my top, which almost slipped completely down and exposed my breasts.

"Man, this is why I don't fuck with yo' ghetto ass, Nae Nae. You always wanna start some shit. Don't come at me with your bullshit right now, man! We done. It's over. Why can't yo' remedial ass get that through your thick mothafuckin' head? And where the fuck is my son at? You betta' not had left him with any of those lame ass mothafuckas you fuckin'!" Jayceon had left my side and was now standing a few inches away from Nae Nae's face as he yelled at her.

I'd seen and had enough. I spun on my heels and left. I was beyond embarrassed as I made my way down the stairs. I thought that I heard Jayceon call out to me as I walked away as fast as I could in my three-inch heels. Let his ass call me. I don't care. With his thot for a baby momma! As I pushed my way through the main entrance to get outside, I heard my name again and felt someone grab my wrist.

I turned around to spew curse words and insults at Jayceon when my eyes fell on Chase!

CHAPTER 9

"*Hey*, hey. What happened? Are you aight?" Chase asked as he took in my slightly disheveled appearance.

I was on the verge of tears and ever so grateful for seeing Chase. "Can you please take me home?" I pleaded with him as I hugged myself because I suddenly felt chilly.

Chase could see my poor physical state and that I was going to have a meltdown. He took his denim jacket off and placed it around my shoulders. He hugged me slightly to him, then I followed his lead as he began walking.

We'd barely walked five steps when I heard an angry voice to the back of me.

"Where the fuck you think you going, Shauntel? You must be out your mothafuckin' mind. You got me fucked up thinkin' you can come with me and roll outta' here with anotha' nigga!"

I turned around to tell Jayceon that he could go straight to hell. When I did, I was greeted with the entire Wu Tang Clan standing behind us. *Oh, hell no!* Jayceon and his crew looked like they were about to kill Chase.

"Shauntel, don't let me tell yo' ass again to get the fuck back here and get in that limo, or I'm gon' fuck homeboy up so bad, he'll be unrecognizable!" Jayceon threatened through gritted teeth.

The look on Jayceon's face made me think twice about continuing with Chase. Jayceon was not playing. I looked at Chase and was about to say that I should go with Jayceon, but Chase wasn't having it.

"Look, I'm not intimidated by him. Let's go. I'll take you home." Chase started walking and attempted to turn me gently so that I could go with him.

In my peripheral vision, I saw Jayceon approaching us. Before I could warn Chase about what was about to happen, Jayceon removed a gun from his waist. Within the blink of an eye, he'd bashed Chase in the back of the head with the butt of his gun. I screamed in horror as I saw the blood instantly flow from the open wound.

I was pushed mercilessly to the side and could do nothing but beg and scream for Chase's life as Jayceon and his squad beat the shit out of him. They were stomping him over and over. Jayceon repeatedly struck him in his face with the butt of his gun.

I ran over and tried to pull Jayceon off Chase. I screamed for him to stop. Chase was rendered unconscious as Jayceon and his boys finally dispersed. I bent down and checked to see if Chase was breathing. His face was a bloody mess. His eyes were swollen and lips busted. He was in bad shape.

I felt hands roughly pull me to my feet away from Chase. "Didn't I tell yo' stupid ass that you was gon' get homeboy fucked up. Don't you ever play with my mothafuckin' emotions, Shauntel! You heard me?" Jayceon's face was inches from mine as he roared in my face and pointed his finger at me.

While the tears rolled down my cheeks, all I could do was nod my head in response.

"Good! Now get your ass in that mothafuckin' limo. I still have to give you your birthday present."

I turned around mechanically and made my way to the limo. I took two steps then heard Jayceon shout to an unconscious Chase, "Mothafucka'! Didn't you get the memo that I'm a mothafuckin' savage?"

*****

I sat in complete silence and ignored the hell out of Jayceon's ignorant ass. We seemed to be driving a further distance than when we headed to the club. I realized that he wasn't dropping me at home. With my head turned, looking out the window, I refused to communicate at all with Jayceon's stupid ass I made a mental note that first thing in the morning, I'd call Chase to make sure he was OK. Jayceon and his crew continued to drink and wild out as music blared in the limo. He wasn't paying me any mind, and that was fine with me. I didn't want to talk to his ass any damn way. This had officially been the worst birthday in history!

When the limo finally came to a stop, my brow creased in confusion when I saw that we were in front of The Ritz-Carlton hotel. Jayceon opened the door and stood waited outside. I made no attempt to move and turned my head in the opposite direction to looking away from him.

"Shauntel! What you think we got all night? Get yo' ass out, man."

Jayceon bent his head and looked at me from the opposite side of the vehicle.

"After what happened at the club with your trifling ass baby momma, and you damn near killing Chase, you better take me home, Jayceon!" I yelled at him while putting on the best angry face that I could.

"Shauntel, if you don't get your stubborn ass out this goddamn limo, I won't hesitate to drag yo' ass up in this mothafucka'!"

I'm not going in that place, I thought as I rested comfortably in the limo, folded my arms, and looked away from him.

Jayceon sucked his teeth and closed the door. Assuming that I'd won, I smiled a little. His crew was still seated in the limo with me. I heard them snickering and whispering, when all of a sudden, my door flung open! I almost fell out as Jayceon grabbed me by my arms, lifted my body, and threw me over his shoulder. He then walked towards the entrance of the hotel.

"Jayceon Clark! If you don't put me down this instant I'm gon' call the police on you!" I shouted at him as I pummeled him on his back with my fists. I could hear his stupid friends hooting, hollering, and laughing. One of them even had the audacity to make the Tarzan call as Jayceon carried me into the lobby. When we reached the front desk, I heard him give the receptionist our names.

Curious onlookers watched and smiled, obviously finding Jayceon's ridiculous display amusing. I planned to go in on his ass as soon as he put me down. After checking in, he walked us towards the elevator and slapped my ass as we entered.

"Jayceon, can you please put me down?" I pleaded with him as soon as the doors closed,

hoping that he would listen.

"You gon' behave? Be a good girl for Daddy?" he said as he slapped me on my ass again.

Even though I was mad at his ass, I was low key getting turned on! I mean, what the fuck was wrong me? Jayceon took me off his shoulder placing me gently on my feet. As soon as he did, I scurried away from him to stand in the far corner and folded my arms while pouting.

He came over to me slowly like a lion about to eat their prey. I quickly turned my head away from him. Standing in front of me, he put his hands on the sides of my face. He then dipped his head to mine.

"Look at me, Shaunie," he said as he nudged his nose gently against my jaw. He started planting soft butterfly kisses on my neck.

And just like that, my temper dissipated, and I turned my face to him.

"You mad with me baby, hmmm?" Putting his hand under my chin, he forced my head up and covered my mouth with his.

I melted against him and opened my mouth as he eagerly pushed his tongue inside. Our tongues clashed. I moaned softly into his mouth and wrapped my hands around his neck. He pushed his body into mine and pressed me into the wall of the elevator. His hands slowly made their way down my stomach, stopping in between my legs. As he started rubbing on me through the fabric of my clothes, the elevator dinged. He pulled away, leaving me breathless. He then reached for my hand and led me out the elevator.

We made our way inside the Suite. This room was no joke! It was huge, with a dining room and living room. The bedroom area housed a luxurious king-sized bed. There were various sofas and seats around the suite. And the bathroom was absolutely breathtaking. It had a rainforest showerhead and could easily hold five people. It even had a spacious bathtub that had lighted candles all around it.

I heard Jayceon close the door behind us as I continued to wander around the suite. I took in a spectacular view of Atlanta while standing by the windows. I felt Jayceon behind me. As he wrapped his hands around me from behind, I faced him.

"Jayceon, are you still involved with Nae Nae?"

He started rubbing his hands up and down my back. Then he took my ear lobe between his lips. I tried my best not to get sidetracked and started pushing on his chest. He stopped and looked at the serious expression on his face.

"Come here, shawty." He took my hand in his and led me over to one of the sofas in the seating area. He pulled me to his lap and placed his hand around my waist. "Look, me and Nae Nae have a son, but that's it. Nae Nae be doin' too much! Shit, I like my girls low key like you, Shaunie. That bitch just mad 'cause I don't want nothing to do with her. Don't let her spoil our time together. This is supposed to be a celebration, remember? In mentioning that, let me give you your gift. Hold up." He reached into his Gucci pants pocket, pulled out a gift box that had the word "Jared's" written on it, and handed it to me.

CHAPTER 10

"*Happy* birthday, baby." He handed me the box and kissed me softly.

I looked at the box and hesitated. My eyes went from the box to Jayceon's smiling face.

"Well? Go on an open up that mothafucka."

I began biting on my lower lip as I removed the lid from the box. I gasped when I looked at the beautiful diamond necklace that lay inside the box. It was made of white gold, and diamonds covered the beautiful heart-shaped pendant. "Jayceon, this is gorgeous. It looks expensive. Thank you." I looked down at him and smiled. Then I pecked him on his lips.

"C'mon, let me spoil you rotten tonight." He pushed my hips gently and guided me to stand. He got up along with me.

As he took the jewelry box out of my hands, he linked our pinkie fingers together as we walked in the bathroom to the tub. Jayceon discarded his leather jacket and pulled his t-shirt over his head. I was sure that my face turned red as I looked down at my feet. The ripples of muscles on his six pack abs had God's Son tattooed them. Seeing him half-naked had me flustered.

"Why you looking at your feet, ma? Come here and take a bath with yo' man."

After hearing his words, my head rose quickly, and I looked at him with surprise. We'd never discussed what we meant to each other. But from the way he'd been acting lately, I could tell he was interested.

"Why you look like you surprised or some shit? I'm not your man now?" Jayceon asked as he walked toward me. He slightly tugged on my jumpsuit and eased it down, exposing my breasts.

Instinctively, I covered my nakedness with my hands and shyly looking away.

"Why you hiding yourself? You do know you sexy as fuck, right? Don't act like you don't know." Jayceon took my hands and moved them aside, exposing my nakedness.

I wasn't being able to watch as he ogled my breasts, so I looked away.

Next, he removed the jumpsuit altogether, and it pooled around my ankles. He bent down to my feet, slipped the heels off, and put them aside. Before standing erect, he placed kisses on my thighs, then my stomach. He then moved my hands away from my breasts, took one of my pink-colored nipples into his mouth, and sucked gently.

My mouth opened, but not a sound came out. I'd never in my life felt anything so wonderful. The way the warmth and wetness of his mouth felt on my nipple rendered me speechless. As he looked into my eyes, he began giving my shoulders a massage. Before I got lost in his sensual manipulations, I decided to set the record straight.

"Jayceon, I didn't plan on having sex with you tonight." I gave him a pleading look, hoping that he would understand. I didn't want him to think I was easy, and give him the wrong impression of me. I had to continue being the good girl that I was brought up to be.

"Nah, I'm not trying to take it there. At least not anymore. The first time I lay this pipe on you, I don't want you to remember shit else but that. All that extra stuff that happened earlier with Nae Nae and that fuck boy you continue to encourage around you, was just too much. But what I am gon' do, is put you in that tub and wash you from head to toe. After that, I'm gon' dry you off with mostly my tongue then the towel, 'till you scream my name and put cum all over my face."

Hearing Jayceon's explicit description of what he wanted to do to me being whispered in my ear, caused wetness between my legs that I was sure would run down my thighs any minute!

Jayceon took the remainder of my clothes off and walked me over to the tub. He signaled for me to get in the tub. I climbed in and sat quickly to hide my nakedness. I watched as Jayceon continued taking the rest of his clothes off. I wanted to look away, but I couldn't. As he stripped off his boxers and stood before me in all his naked glory, I could feel my eyes growing big when I looked at his dick. I'd never seen one before, but I was quite sure that all men weren't as blessed as Jayceon! He was hung. Being a whiz in math, I did a quick estimate of his dick size and came up with about nine inches!

He climbed in the tub with me then pulled me to him so that my back was on his body. Starting with my neck, he began lightly rubbing my body with a washcloth.

Because of the relaxed mood, I took the opportunity to bring up

Chase. I hated had been done to him by Jayceon and his crew, and felt that I needed to address it.

"Jay," I said softly.

"Yeah, bae?"

"I don't think it's cool what you and your friends did to Chase. He's a really nice person." I felt Jayceon's hands go still for a moment as though he was contemplating if he should answer me.

"Homeboy wants to fuck you, Shauntel. Don't get shit twisted. I'm not going to sit back and watch some lame ass make moves on you. Must have me fucked up, man," Jayceon said as he continued washing my stomach.

I bit down on my bottom lip and thought about pushing the issue, but decided against it. I'd already made up my mind that first thing in the morning, I would call Chase and apologize profusely. I hoped he that he'd forgive me.

Because I was deep in thought, I was unaware that Jayceon's hand had slipped between my legs until I felt the cloth rubbing on my pussy. I took my hand and placed it on top his so that he'd stop, but he gently pushed my hand away.

"Relax baby. Let me do me. You gon' be feeling better in no time." He kissed the back of my neck as he continued rubbing the cloth on me.

I squirmed because of my inexperience.

"Open your legs for me baby," he whispered in my ear.

My legs spread open and gave Jayceon free access as if they had a mind of their own.

He discarded the cloth and replacing it with his hand. Then started massaging the sides of my pussy. My breathing became labored as a newfound sensation washed over me.

That wasn't the half of how he made me feel. He found my clit with his index finger and rotated his finger in a slow motion. I gasped loudly and threw my head back. I rested it on his shoulder as I closed my eyes and moaned softly.

"You like that, Shaunie?" Jayceon asked as he kept up with his torturous pleasure.

"Yes." My voice was barely audible as I answered.

"This gon' be my pussy, Shaunie?"

"Yes."

At this point, if Jayceon had asked me to sign my soul over to the devil, I would have! So long as he didn't stop what he was doing.

"From tonight on you gon' be mine and only mine. You hear me, Shaunie?" His finger started moving in quicker circles, and I thought I was about to lose my mind.

"Ye—yes," I stuttered.

"Get yo' ass up and go lay on the bed. I'm 'bout to suck your pussy 'till you start speaking in tongues."

He pushed me off him, and I stood up. With Jayceon's help, I stepped out the tub. Then he followed. He took his sweet time drying me off with the towel, and payed particular attention to my breasts and in between my thighs.

I could barely walk as he led me over to the king-sized bed. He then laid me down.

"You ready? Scream as loud as you want 'cause ain't nobody gon' come save your ass." Jayceon stood before me in all his naked glory and stroked himself as he spoke. "I know you're new to this, so I'm gon' tell you what to do, and you gon' do it, aight"

As I breathed heavily, I nodded to let him know that I was down.

"Nah, you better fuckin' answer me. I'm not OK with that nodding-your-head bullshit."

"OK, Jayceon," I replied shyly as I marveled at the way he stroked his rock-hard erection.

"Touch your breasts for me and play with them nipples." Hesitantly, I did as I was told and looked away from Jayceon's intense gaze as I did.

"Aye, look at me, Shaunie. A nigga don't have time for that shy shit."

Again, I did what I was told and held his gaze as I gently pulled on my nipples. I could feel myself getting wetter by the second as Jayceon continued looking at me while he stroked himself.

"Aight, now rub your pussy."

My hands halted at his request. I was shocked that he could ask me to do such a thing.

"No, Jayceon. I can't do that." I was appalled at what he was asking me to do. I've done it a few times, but never in front of anyone.

"Man, didn't you hear what the fuck I said, Shaunie? Rub on your pussy the same way I did just now."

I closed my eyes then timidly put my right hand against my dripping mound and gently touched myself. I used my index finger like Jayceon had, and rotated it slowly against my pearl. I loved the way it felt and became oblivious to Jayceon standing before me.

"You like how that feel baby?"

"Yes," I replied. I then opened my eyes and looked at him. I couldn't hold back the groan as it passed my lips.

"Bring that ass to the edge of the bed." Jayceon signaled me with his finger.

I scooted to the end of the bed as I watched Jayceon get on his knees. He placed kisses on my upper thighs, then my inner thighs. As he made his way towards my pussy lips agonizingly slow, I held my breath.

He sucked on one side of my pussy, then the other. I groaned loudly at the intense feeling. Taking the tip of his tongue, he flicked my bud in a quick motion, which caused me to squirm. Jayceon's mouth and tongue expertly worked their magic on me. The way he teased, licked, and sucked me made me holler his name countless times. Next thing I knew, I was hit with the most powerful orgasm.

"Damn, Shauntel. You got that honey pussy. You gon' have a nigga hooked for real," Jayceon said as he lapped up my juices.

I covered my face with my hands and waited to come down from cloud nine.

I felt Jayceon lay on the bed. "Come here, baby." He reached for me then moved my hands from off my face and pulled me next him.

As we lay in the spooning position, I turned around to ask, "Ain't I supposed to do something for you in return?" I blushed.

The way his dick was pressed against my back it felt like it was about to drill a hole in me. Therefore, I knew he wanted me, so it was only fair that I reciprocate.

"Nah, I told you, when you get this dick in your life, I want it to be the only thing you remember. Besides, I got control, and your birthday celebration's not over yet," Jayceon said as he kissed my shoulder.

"Huh? What'chu mean it's not over?"

Jayceon chuckled softly behind me. "We're flying to Miami in the morning. My homeboy got a club in Miami also. But this one's a little different than the one that we partied at tonight though."

Jayceon must be out his mind if he thinks that I'm flying with him to Miami. "Jayceon, I just can't fly out to Miami with you. What about my mother? I've never been away from her for very long. I can't go with you," I said while shaking my head. *What'll my mother think? She'll probably feel like I abandoned her something. Nope! I'm not going."*

"Your mom will be just fine. The nurse I hired was not only for tonight. I hired her permanently. Your mother needs special care, Shaunie, and she'll be gettin' just that from now on."

I sat up and looked at him with a stunned expression on my face. "Jayceon, I can't afford to pay a nurse. What are you thinking?"

"Man, lay down. Don't tell me what I can't do. I'll be paying the nurse, damn! Look, from tonight on, you'll need to get used to me helping you out. Just let me do what I do, Shaunie. Now lay back down and spoon with yo' man."

Jayceon tugged on my arm forcefully, and I lay down next to him. This conversation wasn't over. I'm not used to being taken care of. I got this!

CHAPTER 11

$\mathcal{W}$e landed at Miami International Airport early the next afternoon. Jayceon had a pre-packed bag for me at the hotel in Atlanta. When I tried again to back out of this trip by telling him that I had no clothes to wear, he walked into one of the rooms and came out with a Louis Vuitton carry-on bag that had brand new clothes for me. I had no excuse.

When Jayceon went to take a shower, I quickly attempted to call Chase, but my call went straight to voicemail. I prayed that he was OK. I called my mother next who sounded like she was in good spirits. Turns out, she and the nurse had attended the same high school. But graduated different years. She told me to have fun and that she'd see me tomorrow when I got back.

So, there we were making our way from the Miami airport to a car that Jayceon had rented. To my surprise, when we got in, Maliq and Trevor were inside. Jayceon explained to me he doesn't go anywhere without his hitters just in case something was to pop off.

As we made our way to the hotel, my eyes were glued to the scenery of busy Downtown Miami. After we reached our destination at the Hyatt hotel, Jayceon checked us in to a suite.

I proceeded to explore the room when I heard Jayceon say, "Look, me and the boys gotta' few business deals to handle, aight. I'm gon' bounce."

Jayceon must be joking if he thinks that he's just going to leave me alone in a strange hotel, and furthermore, in a strange state!

"So, you just gonna' up and leave me, Jayceon?" I asked looking at him with fire in my eyes.

"Don't start, aight. Go take a swim in the pool or some shit. I picked out a nice bikini for you. It's in the bag." He lifted the Louis Vuitton bag that he'd packed and tossed it on the bed.

I defiantly stared at him and refused to examine the bag

"Man, you hard headed as fuck. I'm out, baby."

Would you believe that he gave me a quick kiss on my cheek and had the audacity to leave my ass! Left me standing there dumbfounded.

"Aaarrrggghhh," I growled to the empty suite. Since I had no choice, I sat on the bed to inspect what Jayceon thought to be acceptable attire for me. I saw matching Victoria Secret underwear sets, a barely-there bikini, and a maxi dress that I assumed was for the return. At the bottom of the bag, however, was a dress that made me wonder who Jayceon had purchased it for. Sure, as hell wasn't for me.

The dress was made of long, sheer material. It was completely see through with a built-in piece that looked like a one-piece bathing suit. *Jayceon must be off his rockers if he thinks I'm wearing that scrap of cloth.* I quickly put it back in the bag as I shook my head.

Exactly five minutes had passed since Jayceon left, and I was officially bored out my damn mind. Then I remembered that I hadn't yet to spoken to Chase. I hurriedly grabbed my phone and dialed his number. After about the fifth ring, I was about to disconnect the call, but he answered.

"Hello?" Chase's voice sounded strained, as if it were a struggle to speak.

"Chase?"

"Who is this?"

It was at that moment that I remembered that I'd never called him or given him my number. Therefore, he had no idea who was speaking to him.

"It's Shauntel." I said I my name as if it were a dirty word because I didn't know if Chase wanted to speak to me.

There was a brief pause before he responded. "Shauntel, are you OK? I was hoping you'd call. Is everything fine? He didn't hurt you, did he?"

Chase's questions amazed me, and they said very much about the individual he was. His condition was horrible because Jayceon and his boys had almost killed him, and yet he wanted to know if I was OK!

"Chase, forget about me. I'm so sorry for what happened. Jayceon and his friends had no right—" Before I could finish my sentence, Chase interrupted me.

"Nah, I'm straight. My friends, who I was at the club with, found me and took me to the hospital. I just got a couple of stitches to the back of my head. It's cool."

Hearing that Chase had gotten stitches, made feel lower than dirt under a rock. I felt like all of it was my fault.

"Chase, I'm so sorry." I apologized to him, again.

"So that's your boyfriend huh?"

I raised my eyebrow at his question, and was nervous about answering him.

"You didn't strike me as the type to be with a street thug, Shauntel."

Was that disappointment that I heard in his voice? Sure as hell sounded like it.

"Look, I know what I'm doing Chase. Don't worry about me," I replied in an attempt to avoid answering his question. "Are you still in the hospital?"

"If I say yes, would you come visit me?"

Chase was full of surprises. But if I was in Atlanta, I would've been his first visitor without a doubt.

"I'm in Miami, Chase." I sounded guilty as hell. Maybe because I'd left Chase practically bleeding to death for my own selfish reasons. It wasn't like I had much of a choice anyway.

"Miami? So, is that what it takes Shauntel? To get your attention, I gotta' have lots of dough and walk around like I'm a billboard advertisement for Gucci?"

What in the hell. Chase doesn't know me like that to be throwing out wild accusations.

"That's not fair, Chase. You don't know me or what I stand for. How dare you judge me by assuming that I'm some sort of a gold digger! I only called to make sure you're OK. You obviously are, so I'll talk to you later."

"Shauntel, wa—" Before his judgmental ass could finish his sentence, he was talking to the dial tone.

My frustrations were on high. Between Chase, and Jayceon leaving my ass in the hotel room, I was pissed. I went to bed and quickly fell asleep.

*****

As Jayceon, Maliq, Trevor and I walked into the club, I adjusted the inner piece of the sheer dress that Jayceon had bought me for about the twentieth time. After having an intense shouting match with Jayceon about the outfit that he'd chosen for me, I had no choice but to give in and put it on.

As I looked around, I realized that this was no ordinary club. No sir! Jayceon wasn't kidding when he said that his friend's club in Miami was different. This fool had brought my ass to a strip club!

I should've known something was off when I saw the name, *Make It Clap*, on the front of the building. I couldn't take my eyes away from the half-naked waitresses. There were two girls performing on stage. The way they climbed up and down those poles, I would've sworn that they came out of their mother's womb swinging from the umbilical cord!

The two women were moving in sync as they did a routine that they'd clearly practiced. Both were covered in tattoos and built like the porn star, Cherokee, with their big booties. The niggas in front of the stage were making it rain hundreds because of the way they made their asses clap!

"Jayceon, why would you bring me up in here?" I asked as I pulled on his t-shirt so that he could come within ear level.

"Cause, I'm about to turn your ass out; bring out that inner freak I know you got inside you," Jayceon replied as he looked deep into my eyes. He gave me a smile that would've made the devil uneasy.

He then took my hand and he led me into a private room with red lights and a loveseat. He had me sit, then told me that he'd be back. Jayceon closed the door behind him as he left.

CHAPTER 12

These disappearing acts that Jayceon has been doing since we got to Miami are getting old, I thought as I sat in the red room alone. As soon as I was about to get up to look for Jayceon, the door opened, and he walked in holding a bottle of champagne with two glasses. He took a seat next to me, opened the bottle, and poured a drink.

I took a couple sips, then put my glass down and whispered to him, "Jayceon, what are we doing in here?" I didn't know why we were the only ones in there.

"Remember when I said that when I lay this pipe on you, I want it to be the only thing you remember about that night?" Jayceon looked at me from over the rim of his champagne glass as he took a sip of his drink.

"Are we gonna' have sex in here?" Good Lord Almighty. I was beginning to feel like I was in a porn movie.

"Nah, but when we're through with this bottle of champagne. My homeboy who owns the club has a surprise for us."

I was totally confused about what the surprise would be, and I gulped my first glass of champagne down with ease. If I'd been paying close attention, I would've noticed that I was doing most of the drinking, while Jayceon did most of the talking. Before I knew it, the bottle was empty, and my ass was lit!

"You ready for the surprise?" Jayceon's hand had somehow found its way under my dress and was rubbing on my pussy.

I was spread eagled on the sofa as I moaned and grinded my hips into his hand. Jayceon stood abruptly, walked to the door, and opened it as I sat panting while awaiting his return.

When the door opened, in walked a female wearing a black lace bra and a black lace thong to match. I tried to adjust myself as best my drunk ass could. Jayceon closed and locking the door then returned to his seat next to me.

"Shauntel, this is Pinkie. Pinkie, meet Shauntel." Jayceon pointed his hand in both of our directions as he made his introduction.

I gave my attention to the female that stood before me. I must admit that she was one exotic-looking woman. She had a caramel complexion, naturally curly hair that stopped at her shoulders, dark brown eyes, a full mouth, and a body like Amber Rose. Paw print tattoos covered her upper thighs.

"Hi, Shauntel. It's nice to meet you. Jayceon said that you're celebrating your birthday," Pinkie said as she extended her hand to me.

I shook her hand and told her that I was.

"Well, at this club we give complimentary birthday dances. Would you like that?"

Not knowing exactly what my response should be, I turned to Jayceon.

He made eye contact with me, leaned in my direction, and put his hand between my legs again. "Would you like that Shauntel?" he asked. His eyes never left mine as he rubbed me on the outside of my panties.

Ignoring the fact that there was someone else in the room with us, I licked my lips hungrily and desired so much more.

"We'll take that as a yes," Jayceon said as he quickly removing his hand and looked at Pinkie.

Because I didn't drink much, the champagne had me feeling a type of way; a very sexual type of way.

Music suddenly filled the red room, and Rihanna's "Love on the Brain" played. Pinkie stood before us, and with a slow motion of her hips and waist, she gyrated to the music. She paid particular attention to me as she danced. I was far from being a lesbian, but looking at the way she whined her hips and the way she looked at me as she did, turned me the fuck on!

Pinkie turned her back to us, backed her ass into me, and gyrated on my lap. In one swift motion, she rocked forward, placed her palms on the ground, and put her ass in the air. Then she slowly made her ass clap.

I turned to Jayceon, and his lust filled eyes said everything that needed to be said. He reached over and slapped Pinkie on her ass---POW! Then holding the back of my head, he kissed me roughly and forced his tongue into my mouth. I moaned lustfully as Pinkie continued her gyrations on my lap.

. . . That's got me feeling this way

It beats me black and blue

But it fucks me so good, and I can't get enough

Must be love on the brain. . .

Rihanna sang in the background.

*****

Jayceon and I were all over each other by the time we got back to the hotel suite. On entering, we were practically ripping each other's clothes off. We kissed with so much aggression that my lips felt swollen. He pinned me against the wall, the got on his knees. Jayceon raised my dress, pulled my one-piece along with my underwear to the side, and hooked my right leg over his shoulder. Diving into my dripping pussy, he sucked on my clit like the world was about to end and this was his final meal.

Someone that didn't know me would never have guessed that this was about to be my first time having sex by the way I was behaving. I couldn't get enough. I rocked my hips forward, placed my hand on the back of his head, and grinded my pussy in his face to demand more.

With one final pull of my bud between his lips, he got up and started unbuckling his Gucci Jeans. "Get on your knees. Let me teach you how to suck this dick, Shaunie."

I freed his length from his boxers, then knelt before him and licked my lips in anticipation.

"Open yo' mouth and don't let your teeth scratch my shit."

I did everything that I was told. Jayceon had me sucking, licking, slobbering, and humming the life out his dick. He coached me until I had him hollering my name. *Not bad for my first time*, I thought as we made our way to the king-sized bed.

"Lay on your back, and open them pretty mothafuckin' legs." He stopped to give my pussy one last flick of his tongue then positioned himself at my entrance.

I held my breath because I knew the pain was going to be unbearable. With just the head of his dick, he bounced gently as I held on to his shoulders. Then he bounced with greater force as I moved my hands to each side of hips; urging him to take his time.

"Look at me, Shaunie." As soon as our eyes connected he gave one final thrust of his hips, entered me, and broke through my virgin skin.

I scratched and grabbed at his back as I repeatedly whimpered in pain. Jayceon stilled for a couple minutes and allowed me to adjust to his size before moving in a slow, sensual in-and-out rhythm. The pain had subsided, and I was now enjoying my first sexual experience. He took his middle finger and rubbed on my clit.

"Aaarrrgggghhh! Fuck, Shaunie. This pussy got mad grip. From this day forward, you mine and only mine. You hear me?"

How was I supposed to answer him when his finger and dick were both doing magical things to my pussy?

"You hear me, Shaunie?" Jayceon asked as he stuck his tongue in my ear.

"Mmmm, ye—yesss, Jay—" My orgasm took over my body so unexpectedly I was unable to complete my sentence.

My body writhed under Jayceon, and he looked into my face as I came extremely hard. That orgasm knocked the breath out of me. Jayceon's pace quickened and he hit all the right spots. He ended up calling out my name and pulling my hair.

We lay joined together as we drifted to sleep. I felt like the luckiest girl in Miami.

But it was the beginning of a complex and twisted love affair.

CHAPTER 13

Six months later . . .

"*B*itch, let this be the last time you call my mothafuckin' phone. I didn't come for you, so don't come for me bitch!" I threw my brand new iPhone on top of the granite countertop in Jayceon's large, spacious kitchen.

The nurse had the day off, so I was preparing lunch for my mother when Jayceon's fucking slut ass baby momma decided to call my mothafuckin' phone. I've had it with that bitch. It'd been the same song and dance with her for the past six months. You'd think her dumb ass would get used to the fact that Jayceon and I were in a relationship and that every weekend, my mother and I stayed at the new townhouse he'd purchased three months ago.

As soon as Jayceon comes down from having his shower, he and I are going to turn into Floyd Mayweather and Oscar de La Hoya. I'm going in on his ass. Jayceon must have me fucked up.

After allowing Jayceon into my life six months ago, it was all good until I began to realize that I was losing myself. I was changing, but not for the better! I was constantly dealing with Nae Nae's disrespectful ass calling my phone. Every other day me and this trick were getting into it despite me changing my number three times, which led me to believe one thing—Jayceon was doing way more than just going over there to check in on his son.

I remembered that when I first met him, I'd received a phone call from her. But being a naïve girl back then, it never dawned on me to ask him how she could've possibly gotten my number. Asking him was useless anyway. He told me that I'm insecure and need to trust him more.

I felt myself slipping further and further down a dark hole. Jayceon had me cursing at him so much that it seemed as if I'd invented new cuss words. The naïve and innocent girl that I was six months ago was no more. When you're involved with someone like Jayceon, you had to learn how to roll with the punches.

On top of that, I had his other bitch to deal with----the streets! I've tried so hard to be understanding. When my stupid ass met him, he was running the "A", so I knew exactly what I was getting into. But that didn't make shit any easier. I started learning more about his street life even though I didn't want to.

I learned about his trap houses, how they operated, and how many dope boys were assigned to each one. I learned the amount of money each trap house was required to make on a weekly business. The most interesting thing that I learned about his operation was the fact that his connect was actually an officer! Yup, a dirty cop. I mean really, who's going to guard the guards?

Jayceon said that he'd met his connect through a trustworthy source over a year ago and that the previous connect had been executed mafia style. I thought it was risky having a cop as a connect, but Jayceon said that he'd come with good recommendations. So, I left it alone.

Jayceon, loved having me and my mother over on weekends. His two-story townhouse was beautiful. We 'd hired nurse to provide my mother around the clock treatment as her body weakened with the cancer that had spread to sixty percent of her body. It was hard to watch as she deteriorated before my eyes. She was completely bedridden for a short while after having her remaining breast removed. She didn't like spending weekends at Jayceon's but had stopped protesting it. I was not going to leave her alone with the nurse at our house. She wasn't fond of Jayceon but he respected that.

"Shauntel! Have you seen the keys for the Range Rover?" I heard Jayceon call out to me as he jogged down the stairs.

I took a deep breath and hoped to not commit murder as I looked at the steak knife that sat on the counter. I swear . . .I almost reached for that fucker! I faced him as he walked into the kitchen. If looks could kill, Jayceon's mother would've needed to plan for his funeral.

"The fuck you lookin' at me like that for?" he asked dramatically and shrugged his shoulders.

"You better put a leash on your baby momma! The next time that bitch calls my mothafuckin' phone, I'm goin' over there, and I'm gonna' stab that ho!" I felt my nostrils flare as I pointed my finger at Jayceon.

"Man, I don't know why you continue to let Nae Nae get under your skin. She's just jealous." Jayceon tried to brush off what I'd said like he always does as if my concerns didn't mean shit to him, which only further pissed me off.

"You think I don't know you still fucking her! How else would she continue to get my new number when I keep changing it?" I moved to stand in front of him.

"You better get the fuck out my face with all that mothafuckin' noise you bringin', Shaunie." Jayceon screwed his face and looked down at me.

I didn't care if he screwed his face till he looked like Flavor Flav. I was sick of this shit. "Jayceon, the day I find out you fuckin' Nae Nae behind my back is the last day I will set foot in this mothafucka. You can quote me on that shit!"

I attempted to move pass him, but he blocked me with his hard, muscular body. I looked up at him and gave him my mean-girl mug.

"You gon' do what? Huh, Shauntel? You gon' do what?

He brought his face to mine, so that our foreheads touched, and then scowled while looking into my eyes. Once upon a time, that would've intimated the fuck out of me, but not anymore.

"I'm going to leave yo—"

Before my sentence was completed, Jayceon grabbed me by my face so hard and squeezed my face with his thumb and index finger. "If you ever think you'll leave this bitch and not come back, you must be out your mothafuckin' mind," Jayceon said as he continued to apply pressure on my face.

I wriggled my face till it was out of his vice grip. "Honestly, Jayceon, sometimes I don't even know why I bother with your ass." I stormed up the stairs as I was on the brink of tears.

I walked into his bedroom and tried to close the door but Jayceon was on my heels. He pushed the door open and walked in. I sat on the bed as tears rolled down my cheeks and felt stupid because, once again, Jayceon's baby momma had gotten the best of me. Jayceon stood in front of me which caused me to look away and avoid eye contact.

"Shaunie, you doin' extra right now with them tears." I rolled my eyes at his words and hurriedly wiped my cheek. Then I got up to attend to my mother.

"Where you goin'? Come here, baby. You know I love you. I don't know why you keep letting Nae Nae upset you. Come here." Jayceon started kissing my neck, then took the tip of his tongue and flicked it on my ear lobe.

"Jayceon, you don't love me. If you did, you wouldn't have your baby momma continuously disrespecting me!" I put my hands on his chest and feebly tried to push him away.

"Stop talking crazy. You know I love you. Let me show you how much."

With those words, he reached for the hem of my dress and pulled it over my head. Then he sat me down, got in between my legs, and forcefully opened them. With his fingers, he rubbed on the fabric of my panties against my fat, aching pussy. I dipped my head back as I waited in anticipation of feeling his mouth on me. He pulled my underwear to the side, spread my lips apart, and flicked his tongue in a quick back-and-forth motion on my clit, which sent shudders through me.

"Aaahhh. Jay, baby, just like that," I moaned as I placed my hand on the back of his head and grinded my sweet pussy in his face.

I swear, Jayceon's head game could make a lesbian turn straight! He was that good. Well, at least to me since I hadn't ever been with anyone else.

Jayceon had my pearl in between his lips and was sucking on it while he moaned as if it was the best thing that he'd ever tasted. After a couple final licks, he went to his feet and roughly turned me around. I was now in the doggy-style position.

"You know what to do! Spread those cheeks for a nigga."

I separated my ass cheeks as I felt Jayceon put the tip of his dick at the opening of my pussy and glided it inside agonizingly slow. He hissed at my tightness as he began to move in and out of me at a quickening pace. I began throwing it back for him because gone was the inexperienced girl. She'd been replaced with a freak in the sheets!

"You gon' leave me, Shaunie? Huh?" Jayceon asked as he slapped my ass, which had gotten fatter since Jayceon and I started fucking.

I shook my head because I couldn't speak.

POW! Jayceon slapped my ass again. Harder this time.

"Fuckin' answer me, Shaunie. You were talking all that shit earlier, now answer me!" Jayceon began pulling my hair as his strokes became more aggressive.

"No, baby. I'm not gonna' leave you. Mmmm."

Jayceon was hitting the fuck out of my G-spot, and I felt like I was about to cum. I buried my face into the sheets, stretched my hands above my head, and bit on my bottom lip as my orgasm rocked my body. He was grunting and pulling on my hair so hard that I thought my scalp would be sore in the morning for sure. Then he grabbed my waist and gave a few final thrusts as he busted inside of me. As he caught his breath, he made slow circular motions with his waist.

I hated myself right now for being stupid. That was all we did----fight then fuck. I was a sucker for his dick.

As Jayceon eased out of me, I felt a little of his cum run out of me and I sucked my teeth.

"Jayceon, you gonna' fuck around and get me pregnant! I keep telling your ass to stop bussin' in me." I wasn't trying to mess up finishing college for anyone.

"You weren't talking that shit a few seconds ago." Jayceon chuckled as he came from the bathroom after cleaning himself off.

I watched as he got dressed and knew that he was about to hit the streets. I couldn't help but feel some type of way. "You about to leave?" I said softly as if I didn't already know the answer.

"Yeah, you know wassup. So, don't even give me them puppy eyes. I'll be back later on tonight. I'll give Nae Nae a call and spit fire on her ass for calling you."

Jayceon grabbed his keys to his custom designed Gucci car since I'd hid the Range Rover keys. Yeah, I know I'm petty. But hey, sometimes you gotta' do what you have to if you want to get your man to keep his ass at home!

CHAPTER 14

"*S*haunie hurry yo' ass up. Why you always late, man!"

I groaned as I listened to Jayceon. I adjusted my short red Gucci tube dress for about the fifth time. Jayceon had me rocking so much designer shit that I could've worn a different outfit each day of the month! I became interested in makeup and hair extensions since I'd gotten with him, even though I didn't need it.

After I walked to my mother's bedroom, I gave her a kiss on her forehead. She was sound asleep. The nurse had fed her and attended to her hygiene, and my mother drifted to sleep a few moments after.

As I made my way downstairs, I had to keep tugging on my dress because it kept riding up my thighs. Fuckin' around with Jay's ass, I'd gained ten pounds! My thighs were thicker, my ass was fatter, and Jayceon loved every bit of it. He said that's what good water does to a body.

We were on our way to his mother's house for their annual family barbeque. I'd become quite acquainted with his family over the past few months. His moms was cool enough. She was always pleasant to me. We weren't best friends or no shit like that, but we kept it classy.

His sister, Jazmine, on the other hand, was my bitch for real! I loved her young, feisty ass. She'd turned sixteen a couple of months ago. Sometimes, I swore she was about twenty! Jayceon would kill for her; he loved that girl with all his heart. She was just eight years old when her father was killed. Jayceon said that after his death, she didn't speak for almost a year.

Jayceon's younger brother, Jahvon, was following Jayceon's footsteps in the street life. He was a couple years younger and was dying to be part of the 'fast money' life like his big brother. But Jayceon said that he would die before he saw his little brother on the streets selling dope. He kept encouraging him to go back to school, but Jahvon wasn't hearing that. Their resemblance was unbelievable! They looked like twins.

"We takin' your car. C'mon." Jayceon had the keys to my BMW X5 in his hands, which was a gift he'd given after he left his phone open and my inquisitive ass snooped and found a bunch of nude photos of some random slut! That's another story.

As we made our way toward the car, Jayceon noticed that I was repeatedly pulling my dress down and laughed.

"Something funny Jay?" I asked as I hopped in the car.

"That ass gon' need its own zip code." Jayceon said, messing with me as he started the car and laughed at his own joke.

Ignoring his ass, I put on my seat belt, sat back in my seat, and prepared to enjoy the ride. On our way, a thought came to mind. I opened my mouth as I looked at Jayceon, but decided that I shouldn't even think to ask such a ridiculous question. So, I turned my attention forward again. Jayceon would have to be a crazy person if he invited

Nae Nae's ass. From what he told me, she was supposed to drop their son off and that was it.

We pulled up to his mother's crib in Glenwood Park, which is a quiet neighborhood that Jayceon had relocated his family to a couple years ago. The house was a modern four-bedroom home that had a spacious backyard where the barbeque was being held. We got out, and Jayceon grabbed the potato salad that I'd volunteered to prepare because, according to Jayceon, my potato salad was the best in Atlanta.

We went to the backyard, and Jayceon headed to the table where there was a shit load of food! You would've thought Ms. Clarke was feeding the entire U.S. Army. There was every type of chicken anybody could think of—grilled, fried, Chinese-styled, stewed chicken, and barbequed. There was yellow, white, and fried rice, and my potato salad was the third one.

I left Jayceon's side when I saw his mother chatting with some other women. Ms. Clarke was a forty-five-year-old, heavyset woman that had the prettiest face, but the saddest pair of brown eyes. Jayceon said that after his father died, she'd vowed to never re-marry. And she'd made good on her promise.

I approached her, wrapped my arms around her, and kissed her cheek. "Hey Ms. Clarke, you're looking good. How've you been?" I asked as we ended our embrace and smiled at each other.

Now, remember when I said that we kept it classy, but weren't best friends? You see, Jayceon's mother was one of those mothers where nobody was ever good enough for her son. In her eyes, Jayceon did no wrong and he was the perfect son. Of course, she knew about Jayceon's lifestyle. Hell, he'd taken over from her dope-dealing husband! But she turned a blind eye to the fact that he was in the streets doing dirt! I knew that she never really approved of me, but anybody was better than Nae Nae's ass, I guess.

"I'm fine, Shaunie. It's nice that you could make it. Go fix yourself a plate. God knows you could use to put some meat on them bones, honey."

I laughed softly and waved her off as I walked away. Was she for real? My fat ass could barely walk in the dress I had on without it riding up my thighs. Ms. Clarke was tripping.

"Hey, Matika." I greeted Maliq's girlfriend as I went back to the table to fix a plate.

Matika was the only person that I hung out with. She and Maliq had started kicking it a month after Jayceon and I met. Since Jayceon never went anywhere without Maliq and Trevor, it was only natural that Matika and I had become friends. She was a beautiful girl, and I didn't know what she saw in Maliq's ass. But then again, maybe she said the same about Jay and me. She looked as if she could've been from Hawaii; she had long, straight hair that stopped at her ass, tanned skin, and slanted eyes. She had a big booty with disproportioned thighs, which made me believe that her ass was fake.

"Have you seen Jay?" I asked her as I scanned the backyard. I wanted to know if he was ready to eat so I could fix him a plate.

"You know how those three are; he, Maliq, and Trevor went out front a couple minutes ago."

Matika was putting so much food on her damn plate that it

started to cave in the middle. *This bitch sure could eat*, I thought as I put some potato salad on my plate.

I was wondering what the three musketeers were up too because lord knows, when they get together, they created a tornado. Matika and I had broken up countless fights at clubs with Jay and his crew. These fools didn't know how to act once that Hennessy got in their system. Hell, I should've known since I was a witness when they damn near killed Chase.

I sighed as Chase came to mind. We'd lost touch after our last conversation where he basically called me a gold digger. I always wondered about him.

"Shaunieeeeee!"

I turned around to the sound of someone screaming my name. Jayceon's little sister, Jazmine, came galloping towards me. I quickly put my plate down so that she wouldn't knock it out of my hand and waited for her to pounce into my arms. Jazmine knocked the wind out of me as she hugged me. I laughed as I pulled her away from me and examined what she was wearing.

"Yo, Jazmine. You better go change before Jayceon has a heart attack." Jazmine was wearing short booty shorts, a very tiny tube top, and a pair of blue Prada sneakers. She rocked a short curly weave. Every two weeks, Jayceon would take her to get her hair and nails done.

"Please, Jayceon can't tell me shit," she said as she twirled so I could get a good look at her outfit.

I noticed that Jayceon's son was nowhere to be seen. I assumed Nae Nae didn't bother to bring him since I would've been there.

"Hey, where's Jahvon? I haven't seen him since I got here." Jahvon was a rebel without cause. He always seemed to get himself into all sorts of trouble.

"Momma sent him to get some ice like an hour ago. You know how he do," Jazmine said as she shook her curly hair. She started making a plate along with me and Matika.

About half an hour after arriving, the barbeque was in full swing. Everyone was enjoying themselves and having a good time. The DJ played strictly old school hip hop. Jayceon's mother said that she didn't understand what the shit rappers nowadays were rapping about. Jayceon and I were dancing to Montell Jordan's song, "This Is How We Do It."

When I noticed that Jazmine kept waving her hands to get my attention, I looked across at her with a perplexed look. Then she pointed in the direction of the back door. Standing there was Nae Nae with her son on her hip.

CHAPTER 15

I stopped dancing briefly and turned around to look at Jayceon who also was looking at Nae Nae. He turned his eyes to me and saw the fire that blazed. He then started walking towards her.

"Jay, where are you going? We're dancing. Jazmine will go get your son."

"Aight, cool. Shake that ass girl."

Jayceon and I continued dancing and ignored the hell out of Nae Nae, who obviously didn't appreciate being ignored by Jayceon while standing with their son. I saw her walk over to us and prepared for the drama and attention that she loved!

"So, you don't see me standing there with *our* son." She stressed the word 'our' as if it were news to me that they shared a son.

"Aye, yo, Jazmine. Come get lil' man real quick!" Jayceon yelled to Jazmine, and she came jogging over.

As she pulled her son away from Jazmine's outstretched hands, Nae Nae fixed her eyes on me and sucked her teeth. "So, your little college bitch is here, and all of a sudden you can't take your own damn son?" Nae Nae sucked her teeth again in annoyance.

I took a deep breath and looked away. I refused to let her get the better of my emotions. Not this time.

We started to get other guests' attention. A few of them were looking at us, including Jayceon's mother who didn't look pleased at all.

"Don't go disrespecting my girl. Fuck around and get dropped right where you stand, Nae Nae! Gimme my damn son." With those words, he took Jaden and handed him over to Jazmine who took him and walked away.

"Talking all that shit. Let this trick know where your dick and mouth were last night. All up in my pussy with your punk ass." Nae Nae waved her fingers back and forth in my and Jay's face and laughed.

Now, I didn't know if she was speaking the truth, but I still felt a type of way about with what she'd said. "Bitch, whose mouth? And whose dick? In which pussy? You must got me fucked up. Don't nobody want any of your stank pussy, Nae Nae.

"Man, get the fuck on. You dropped my son off, so you can bounce now!" Jayceon pointed in the direction of the door.

"Oh, I got your bitch!"

You'd think that she was about to go after Jayceon, right? Wrong! This scandalous bitch lunged at me and grabbed my hair. She didn't get a hold of me for too long before Jay grabbed her and pushed her ass off me so hard that she fell flat on her ass.

"Jayceon, Nae Nae, and Shauntel! I am trying to have a peaceful barbeque with my friends and family. You all need to gone with all that bullshit, now!" Ms. Clarke came over and stood between me and Jayceon as Nae Nae was left with the task of picking her stupid self off the ground.

I fixed my hair, and as I was about to apologize a little light-skinned guy that looked to be about seventeen years old, came running to us.

"Yo, Jayceon. You need to get your ass down to the precinct man. Jahvon just got arrested."

"I knew it was a matter of time before I'd hear those words. I just knew it!" Ms. Clarke placed her hands on top of her head and continuously shook her head.

"Fuck! Yo, what the fuck did he do man?" Jayceon shouted as he placed a hand on his mother's shoulders and tried to calm her down.

"I'm not sure. One of the guys that he was kicking it with just called me and told me let you guys know."

"Mom, don't worry, aight. Let me go and see wassup. C'mon, Shaunie. Let's go." He grabbed my hand as we made our way past an irritated Nae Nae who'd finally managed to get up from off the floor.

Jayceon and I got into the BMW and made our way over to the police station.

*****

As we entered the station, Jayceon took off ahead of me and made his way to the front desk where a middle-aged black officer with a thick mustache sat. He was on the phone, so Jayceon waited until he got off.

"I'm looking for a Jahvon Clarke. He got arrested a little while ago."

The officer looked at Jayceon and then at me with a blank expression on his face. "What was he arrested for," the officer asked dryly. He looking as if all he wanted was to get home and crawl into bed.

"I don't know why he got arrested. That's what I need to find out."

Knowing my man and the fact that he's easily irritated, I put my hand on top of his.

"Could you please find out? We'll have a seat while you do," I said as I took Jayceon's hand in mine and lead him over to the sitting area.

A couple of minutes passed, and the officer behind the front desk summoned us over. "OK. Mr. Clarke was arrested for possession of an illegal firearm and for having weed on his person. The charge of marijuana possession can be dropped, as he was found with a small amount. However, we will have to charge him with possession of an illegal fireman." With that being said, the officer went back to whatever he was doing as if we weren't still standing there.

"Well, can I at least see him?" Jayceon asked the officer who looked as if he was becoming annoyed.

"I don't think that's possible, but let me check. Please, have a seat." We made our way once more to the seating area.

"This is not good, Jay. You know the system doesn't work for black people. They're gonna' sink his ass. He'll do a lot of time for this shit," I said as I looked at him.

Just then, about four officers walked in, which grabbed the attention of Jayceon. "Not if I can help it. Wait here." I watched as Jayceon got up and made his way towards the officers. He pulled one of them aside, and they spoke to each other.

As I looked on, it seemed as if they might know one another by the way they were interacting. The officer looked to be in his late forties with a rich chocolate complexion. If I was into older men, he could get it. They talked for about ten minutes then I saw Jayceon pointing at me as he made his way across.

"I'm gonna' go see him, aight. I'll be right back." He gave me a quick kiss on my cheek as the officer that he'd been talking to came up to him. They walked to the elevator and got in.

I was starting to get a bit restless when after thirty minutes, Jayceon and his younger brother made their way out the elevator. I didn't know who looked more pissed, Jayceon or Jahvon. I got up and walked towards them, then we all walked out the door. I don't know what Jayceon had did or said to the officer that he'd talked to, but whatever it was, it worked.

On our way to drop Jahvon off at his mom's house, I learned that all of his charges had been dropped. Just like that as if it were magic!

"Man, if your stupid ass continues to be on this bullshit, you gon' fuck around and end up prison, and I won't be able to help your ass!" Jayceon shouted at his brother who was sitting in the front seat.

"I don't need you to babysit me, Jay. I got this!" Jahvon said coolly like we didn't just get his ass out of a police station.

"You got this? Nigga, you ain't got shit. You lucky I know that fucking officer back there, or yo' dumb ass would still be sitting there waiting for them to take your ass to jail."

As I listened to Jayceon, I was confused as hell. I mean, it's OK for Jayceon to run the streets, but he didn't want his brother doing the exact same thing that he does.

Jayceon shouted at his brother the entire ride home. But I thought that he should've kept all that air in his lungs because Jahvon's ignorant ass sat there slouched and ignored the fuck out of his big brother.

CHAPTER 16

*I*t had been a week since the scenario with Jayceon's brother, and there wasn't a day that Jayceon didn't go to his mom's place to check on him. He said that he owed it to his father to make sure that his brother and sister were safe.

This day was the same. I'd left class when Jayceon called me to let me know what time he'd be home after he left his mom's house. Matika and I had planned to meet to hit up the mall and get our nails done.

I decided to quit my part-time job at the coffee shop with Jayceon convincing me that I should, of course. He said that all my free time should be spent studying or being with my mother, so I agreed and quit.

After shopping, Matika and I sat in the food court and ate a couple of Cinnabons. Matika pulled out her phone and called Maliq to see if he could come get her, but his phone rang out. "This nigga gets on my goddamn nerves when he don't pick up my calls," she said as placed her phone back into her Steve Madden handbag.

I was ready to get the hell out the mall, but I couldn't just leave her there. The thing is that Matika lived with Maliq, and Maliq lived in a pretty bad part of Georgia. Jayceon would get in my ass if he knew that I even considered going over there to drop Matika off. Against my better judgement, I said to myself, *fuck it!*

"Come on, girl. I'll give you a lift home," I told her as I grabbed the stuff I'd bought.

"Are you sure? I could just keep trying Maliq 'till he answers."

I stood up and gave her a look that said she was being silly. "Look, it's no trouble. I'm ready to go on home anyway, and I just can't leave you here. So, let's go, girl," I said while smiling at her.

She got up and followed me out the mall. "Girl, can I ask you something?" Matika said as we left the parking lot and headed onto the freeway. "OK, listen. What should I do if I can't take the dick size that Maliq has?"

I was a little confused by what she was asking, so I asked her to elaborate. "What'chu mean? Is he too big or too small?" I asked with a crease in my forehead. We came to a stop at a red light, and I turned and looked at her.

"Girl, that nigga is hung like a horse! The first time we had sex, I was like, 'nigga where in the hell is that gonna' fit?'"

Me and Matika burst out laughing. This is what you called grown folks problems.

"Well, Jay's big and all, but not freakishly big. I can handle what he's working with. The best advice that I can give your ass is inebriate and lubricate! You better keep those bottles of Hennessy and KY Jelly in stock, girl."

We continued laughing and chatting it up as I pulled up to the projects where she lived with Maliq.

"Thanks for the lift, girl. I appreciate it. You better get goin' before Jayceon find out you were over here, even though it's just 7:00."

I smiled at her as she reached to collect her stuff that was laid out in the back seat. After seeing that she had everything, I unlocked the doors so she could get out. "It's no problem. Don't forget, we hittin' up the club this weekend, aight."

"Oh, lord. I just hope we don't get our asses kicked out of this one! I swear we been kicked out just about every club in the "A" because of Maliq and them."

We both chuckled as she opened the door to climb out. The chain of events that happened next was all a blur.

As soon as Matika opened the door, out of nowhere, a guy dressed in all black appeared and pointed a gun in her face. Next, my door was flung open and I now I had a gun pointed in my face also.

"Y'all two bitches know what the fuck this is. Hand over them mothafuckin' handbags."

I believe we were in shock because neither of us attempted to move and give up what was asked of us.

"What the fuck. You bitches slow? Hand me the mothafuckin' handbags." The guy who had the gun trained at Matika, screamed at us, and all of a sudden----SLAP! Matika was dealt a vicious slap to her cheek.

"Why you hit her! Look, chill. Aight. We'll give you what you asked for." I looked over at Matika who was rubbing the side of her face. She looked scared as hell.

"Bitch, what you say," the guy on my side said to me as he grabbed my hair and tugged it so hard that I thought my hair was about to come out in his hand.

"You got a real smart mouth. If I had some more time, I'd put that mouth to use you fucking bitch! Now hand me those mothafuckin' bags."

Matika and I did what we were told. We were then ordered to place our hands in front of us as they took all our jewelry off our hands. However, as I was being relieved of my belongings, I stole a quick glance and saw a very unique tattoo on his neck. I made a mental note of it.

"Where your cell phones at?" We handed over those next. They roughly snatched our phones out our hands, then Matika and I waited for what was about to happen next. I didn't know about Matika, but I was praying; asking that God didn't let these guys end my life because I was all that my mother had.

"Now, you two hoes count to mothafuckin' ten before I bore a hole in y'all fucking brains," the guy on my side said to us as he forced the barrel of the gun into my mouth.

As soon as he removed it, Matika and I started counting to ten in unison like preschoolers as the guys ran off with our stuff. ". . . eight . . . nine . . . ten." After completing our countdown, we looked around nervously, but the guys were nowhere in sight.

"Matika, hurry up and get inside!" I shouted. I was scared for both of our safety. When Jayceon hears about this, he'll kill my ass! I'm going to get called hard-headed and stubborn, and told that I'm not able to follow simple instructions. I'm certain that he'll be calling my phone any minute to find out where I'm at. And when I don't pick up, he's going to be pissed!

"Shit! Those two are lucky that I don't know their faces, or Maliq would've killed their ass," Matika said as she continued rubbing the spot on her face that she'd gotten slapped.

Oh, it's obvious that she wouldn't have recognized them. Any fool who lived around there would know not to fuck with Maliq or anyone or anything that pertains to him. So, these guys were definitely not from around there.

"Don't worry, I got a good look at the neck tattoo on the guy who was pointing the gun at me If I ever see it again, I'll know it's him." I would remember that tattoo anywhere because I'd never seen one like it before.

"OK, good. Get home safe, aight," Matika said as she got out my car.

As soon as she jumped out, I locked my doors as fast as I could. Matika bolted for the apartment building. I sped off and made my way to Jayceon's house while saying a prayer out loud this time. Lord knows that I was going to need it!

*****

After pulling into the driveway at Jayceon's house, I stepped inside the house. It was in completely dark which led me to believe that Jayceon had fallen asleep early. I barely took two steps up the stairs when I heard a voice in the corner of the room.

"Where the fuck were you, Shauntel? I've been calling your phone for the past ten minutes."

Jayceon made my heart skip two beats; sitting in the corner of the living room like a mothafuckin' ninja or some shit! After stuttering ever so softly that I'd gotten robbed, Jayceon asked me to repeat what I'd said.

"Yo, what the fuck did you just say?"

"I said that I got robbed, Jay." I was looking down at my hand as I twisted it until it hurt, while I waited for him to go off.

Jayceon reached in front of me; not to comfort my ass, but to get in my face so he could yell at me as if I were his child. "The fuck you mean, you got robbed?" Last I knew, you were with Matika, and I know your stupid ass ain't dumb enough to go over where Matika live at."

Silence in the house because we both knew the answer to that question! Jayceon pulled his head back when I didn't answer his question.

"Shauntel, you mean to tell me you were over on that side of town?"

I was finally able to look up at him so that I could begin to explain myself. "Jay, Matika was trying to call Maliq, but he wasn't picking up his phone. So, I offered to drop her off. How was I to know that we would've gotten robbed, Jay?" I said as I tried to defend my actions. "I mean, it's not like I could've just left Matika there!

"How were you to know? 'Cause I told your mothafuckin' hard-headed ass not to ever go over there. That's how! Man, you don't ever listen to simple instructions. If you would've called me, I'm pretty sure you would've known that Maliq was rolling with me. That's my hitter; he always with me. Now, because you don't know how to listen, those two mothafuckas gon' be two dead niggas before the week is out. Their mothers gon' be plannin' their funerals. Best believe that. Tell me everything that happened, and don't leave out one single mothafuckin' detail!"

Jayceon led me over to the sofa where we sat down, and I recounted everything that had taken place. Jayceon clenched his jaw as I repeated to him about being called a bitch, having the gun put in my mouth, and being told that he would put my mouth to use.

"You sure you'll remember the tattoo if you see it again? And if you hear his voice again, you're gonna' to remember that too?"

I nodded in response. My memory was on point. I knew for a fact that I'd remember those important details if I ever came face to face with him again, which I doubted that I would. I mean, what would be the chances?

CHAPTER 17

"*If your dude come close to me, he gone wanna ride off in a Ghost with me.*

I might let your boy chauffeur me, but he gotta' eat the booty like groceries."

I sang the lyrics of Jhene Aiko's verse in the song, "Post to Be", in Jayceon's ear as we danced in the VIP section of his friend's club. This was maybe the only club in Atlanta that Jayceon and his boys were still allowed to enter.

"You know I'll eat that booty all damn night, Shaunie," Jayceon whispered in my ear as he licked my neck with the tip of his tongue.

This right here was what I appreciated; when my man and I could kick it and enjoy each other's company. Well, with the exception of six of his friends and Matika. All of whom were present in the VIP section.

If Jayceon could understand just how much I loved him. I loved him way more than the streets ever would. But I was his mistress; the streets had his heart!

"Babe." I had my arms wrapped around Jayceon's neck as I looked into his eyes.

"Yes," Jayceon replied, then kissed and sucked hard on my neck.

My clit pulsed with lust partly because of all that damn Hennessy Black I'd consumed. I was horny as hell. "You love me, Jay?" I took my hands and held his face; forcing him to look at me as he answered. My mother always said that the eyes are the windows to your soul. If you want to know how somebody really felt about you, all you had to do was look them dead in the eyes.

"You know I love you, bae. Even though you don't ever listen to a nigga, with yo' big head."

I swatted him playfully on his shoulder. I lifted my head and kissed his lips, then greedily pushed my tongue in his mouth. I swear, Hennessy was like an aphrodisiac for my ass. I put my hand between us and caressed the bulge in Jayceon's pants that I was no doubt responsible for.

"Show me how much you love me, and fuck me right here, Jayceon." I practically begged as I bit hard on his lower lip and continued rubbing on his dick, which I wanted to feel inside of me.

"Yo, your ass could never handle your liquor for shit," Jayceon said and chuckled. He ran his hand under my barely-there skirt that stopped a little below my ass.

"Please, daddy?" I said, then placed butterfly kisses on his neck as I groaned softly and rubbed myself up on him.

Now, if someone had told me six months prior that I'd be standing in a club, begging for the dick, I would've told that person to go fuck themselves! But nevertheless, here I was.

"Think I'm gon' say no to some pussy like a punk? Let's go downstairs." He took hold of my hand, and we made our way downstairs.

But first Jayceon stopped to let Maliq and Trevor know that he'd be right back because they would've been sure to follow.

We couldn't have reached the inside of Jayceon's Gucci Maybach fast enough. The windows were tinted just right so we wouldn't be seen from the outside. As soon as we climbed in the back seat and closed the door, I was ripping Jayceon's clothes off. Jayceon laughed at my eagerness, but I really couldn't have cared less. I unzipped his pants and freed his rock hardness. My mouth watered from the desire to taste him.

Taking the tip of my tongue, I swirled it in a circular motion over his head and made him groan from deep within his stomach. I then placed my full lips over his shaft and took every sweet inch of him into my mouth. I took my time and enjoyed the feel and taste of him.

Jayceon hissed as I expertly sucked on him and took in all nine inches of pleasure. I bobbed my head and groaned as I took great joy in servicing his dick just like he taught me.

"You know I like it extra wet Shaunie; spit on my dick," Jayceon said with a fistful of my hair, extensions included, wrapped in his hand.

Doing as I was told, I spit a generous amount of saliva out on his dick and slurped it right back up. With his hand still in my hair, Jayceon pulled me up and placed my back against the door. With one leg propped on the seat and the other on the ground, he wasted no time diving into my juicy pussy.

With one lick, I was calling out his name. I placed one hand on the back of the passenger seat and the other on the window behind me. Jayceon flicked his tongue tip on my clit in a quick back and forth movement. My orgasm came so quickly and unexpectedly that I grabbed onto his shoulders as if I were afraid to fall from an unseen height.

"Oh fuck, Jay. That was so fucking good," I said as he positioned me so that I was now straddling him. He eased me down onto his nine inches of pleasure! Me and Jay were rocking the hell out of that Maybach as we fucked under the influence.

Afterward, we made our way back to the entrance of the club; holding hands and giggling like a couple of teenagers. As we stood behind two guys at the entrance, something got my attention. The guy in front of me said something to his friend, and there was something about his voice. I couldn't put my finger on it. I looked at him a little closer and almost choked on my spit! My eyes focused on a butterfly tattoo that wasn't actually a butterfly; the body of the butterfly was made to look like a penis, and the wings were well-crafted women.

I remembered that tattoo all too well. The two guys walked inside the club, and as Jayceon attempted to move forward, my feet stayed glued to the floor. He looked over at me with a look that asked what my problem was. Jayceon tugged my hand which prompted me to move. I was wracking my brain thinking about if I should mention to Jay that the guys who robbed me and Matika a few days ago were at the club!

CHAPTER 18

*J*ayceon and I climbed the stairs and made our way back to the VIP section to meet up with his crew. I gently tugged his elbow so that he could bring his head down. I spoke in his ear as I told him that I needed to holla at Matika real quick and that I'll be back.

Matika and Maliq were sitting on a couch and sucking and fondling on each other as I approached. I stood in front of them a few seconds before she finally looked up at me. I waved to her and signaled her to come with me. She stood and walked over.

"You won't believe who's here, Matika!"

She gave me a puzzled look and shrugged her shoulders.

"The guys who robbed us; I just saw them entering the club. I made out his tattoo and I heard his raspy voice. I know it's him!"

Matika's eyes grew wide as she looked at me in shock. "Let's tell Maliq and them. They gonna' fuck those fools up for real!" Matika started to turn and walk toward Maliq to relay to him what I'd just told her, but I quickly grabbed her by her elbow.

"Girl, do you think that's a good idea? They gone cause mayhem in this club. We know they all strapped plus they drunk as hell. This could end pretty bad, Matika." I mean, I wanted nothing more than to see those guys get dealt with, but not if it may cause innocent people to get hurt. The club was packed. And Jay and his crew were packing heat since their friend owned the club had no problem letting them in strapped. Things could go from zero to one hundred real quick!

"So, we just gonna' stand here and let those fools party up? That mothafucka slapped me, Shaunie! Let's go see if we can spot them." She took hold of my hand, and we made our way toward the railing where we could easily look at the crowd below. "You see them?" Matika asked as my eyes roamed the party goers.

"There they go right there," I said as I spotted the guys standing by the bar ordering drinks. *Those fools were probably paying for their shit with our money that they'd stolen.*

I swear on everything that I didn't realize that Matika was no longer at my side. By the time I looked to my left to tell her that we should get back so we wouldn't look suspicious, Matika was sitting on Maliq's lap, whispering in his ear. By the way his face contorted as she spoke to him, I knew without a doubt that she was singing like a canary! *Shit!*

I didn't know it was possible to hear your own heart beating in a club that was full of people and loud ass music. But that's exactly what was happening to me as I saw Maliq push Matika off his lap. His eyes made contact with mine, briefly as he stood and made his way over to Jayceon who was talking to Trevor.

I raced over to Matika to get in her ass. "What the fuck, Matika! Why you had to go and say anything," I yelled as I grabbed her upper arm.

She pulled away from me roughly. "Those mothafuckas need to be dealt with! That fool slapped me, not you. Let the crew deal with this and stop being a little bitch!" She looked at me angrily then turned and walked away.

I turned my attention back to Maliq. I could tell that he'd just finished letting Jayceon and Trevor know what was up because the look Jayceon gave me as his eyes fell on mine, could've turned me turn to stone.

Jayceon came storming over to me. I cowered back as he grabbed hold of my arm and practically dragged me over to where Maliq, Trevor and Matika were standing.

Looking down at the crowd, he said, "Fuckin' show me where the fuck they at. So, were you planning on letting those fools just party and have a good ass time, and not lettin' me know they were here? Huh, Shauntel? I'm gon' deal with yo' ass when we get home." Jayceon's mouth was against my ear as he spoke through clenched teeth.

This was definitely the first time I did what the fuck I was told without being asked twice! I pointed out those two guys before I could even blink.

"Let's go!"

With those final words, I watched as Jayceon, Trevor and Maliq make their way downstairs into the crowd and head to the bar. I looked at Matika who was standing next to me, and she had a smile on her face. Maybe she was used to this type of shit, but I certainly was no. Even though this wasn't the first time these three had caused problems in a club, this situation was different because it was personal.

Jayceon and his crew surrounded the two guys. But before they reached them, I saw Trevor reach for his gun at the small of his back, and he now had it pressed against the nigga with the butterfly tattoo on his neck. It seemed to me that Jayceon spoke to him ever so calm and cool. Next, I saw all of them walking towards the exit, but not before Jay looked at VIP section and signaled to me. Maliq did the same to Matika.

I wasn't sure what was going to happen, but I was certain that I wasn't going to like it one bit! Matika grabbed my hand and we went down the stairs and exited the club. After we got to the parking lot, we found Jay and his crew in a far corner. The three had their guns pointed at the two niggas that had robbed us.

"Come over here, baby." Jayceon nodded his head at me.

I walked over slowly and stood next to him.

"You know these two mothafuckas right here?" he asked.

But I refused to look at them. I kept my eyes on Jayceon as I shook my head.

"You know I hate when you don't answer me, baby. Take a look at these two pussy niggas and tell me if you know them. Go on, take a look."

I turned my head and made eye contact with my robber. He gave me a look as if he was trying to let me know that I better not identify him.

"Yeah! These two fuck boys robbed us," Matika said. She looked like she was about to attack the nigga that slapped her, but Maliq held her back.

"Before we go any further, I want you to apologize to my girl right here." Jayceon took me and hugged my waist.

What the hell was wrong with him?

"She said that you called her out of her name. I believe the word you used was "bitch." Is that right, baby?"

I knew his question was rhetorical, so I kept my ass quiet.

"Now, I want you to be a real good boy and apologize to her." Jayceon removed his hand from around my waist and put it behind his back with his other hand still pointing the gun straight at the robber's chest.

"Nigga fuck you and your BITCH!"

This fool clearly doesn't see that his stupid ass is outnumbered. Why couldn't he just do what he was told? I knew that look I saw in Jayceon's face all too well, so I took two steps away from him.

"That was so disrespectful," Jayceon said a little too calmly. He used the gun to bash that nigga's face. The crack sound that I heard, and the blood that followed, let me know that his nose was broken. Tattoo guy crumpled to a heap on the ground, which was pretty stupid because he was then dealt a swift kick to his face by a pair of retro Jordan's!

"Aaarrrggghhh! Fuck, man. Aight, I'm sorry! I'm sorry," he apologized as he held onto his nose which was leaking all over his white Polo t-shirt.

"Man, get your bitch ass up!" Jayceon screamed with the gun pointed at him.

He staggered to his feet while still nursing the injury that had been inflicted to his nose.

"Take a good look at my girl and apologize like you mean that shit before I pump your body with lead nigga. APOLOGIZE!" The gun was now pointed to him again.

Tattoo guy looked at me with blood covering most of his face and mumbled an apology. "I'm sorry for calling you a bitch," he said as he grimaced in pain.

Now what? I thought as I looked at Jayceon.

"And which one of you slapped my girl?"

Everyone's attention now went to the other guy who was standing there looking like he was constipated. You could tell this nigga was shook by the amount of sweat on his face!

"Not so tough now, are you? You fuckin' pussy!" Matika surprised the hell out of me when she pulled her hand back and slapped the shit out of dude. It wasn't enough though because his face didn't even move.

"Nigga, didn't yo' momma ever tell you not to hit a female?" Maliq said.

I believe he was about to say he was sorry when----POW! Maliq shot him in the chest.

"Yo, what the fuck, Maliq!" Jayceon said as he looked in Maliq's direction.

Before Jayceon could utter another word, a second shot rang off. POW! This time it was Trevor that fired the shot and hit tattoo guy in the side of his neck. They both slumped to the ground as they bled out.

"You two mothafuckas have zero chill, man. We were supposed to take them somewhere, not shoot them where there are witnesses and shit! Y'all sloppy asses gon' fuck around and make us catch a case. Man, clean this shit up. And make sure when you're done, nobody can find their bodies."

Jayceon and the guys placed their guns back in their waist. Jayceon took hold of my hand and led me to his car. Maliq's all-black heavily-tinted Land Rover was parked next to us.

We left Maliq and Trevor cleaning up the mess that they'd made. We had Matika with us so we could drop her off at home. I hoped that night didn't come back to bite us in our ass at some point. I couldn't even bring myself to look over at Jayceon. I was numb. *I was now a witness to not one murder, but two! Is this what he does when he's out in the streets?*

Jayceon was completely unconcerned. He took a cigarette and lit that shit up, then turned on the radio. Out of all the songs he could've chosen to play, his choice was DMX's "Party Up."

"Y'all gon' make me lose my mind, up in here, up in here . . ."

I was looking at Jayceon incredulously as he sang along and bobbed his head in time to the song. He blew smoke out the window as he puffed on his cigarette.

As I looked away from him and focused my eyes on the road, I couldn't help but think that Jayceon was more than just someone who runs the ATL. He was also someone you did not want to cross because if you did, he would make you regret it!

CHAPTER 19

I was at home studying for an exam while Jayceon was out doing God knows what in the streets. It had been a week since the club fiasco, and believe me when I say that I never brought up that incident after it happened. Number one: I was so scared out of my damn mind about what I'd seen that I didn't sleep properly until the sixth night after the incident. And number two: I didn't want to risk Jayceon thinking that I didn't have his back. To some, that may seem stupid. But love can make you do stupid things, I guess.

I sucked my teeth as I felt a vibration. I looked at my phone as it vibrated against my bed. I saw the word "unknown" and shook my head. It baffled the fuck out of me that no matter how many times I got a new number, Nae Nae always seemed to get it just so she could pest the hell out of me. I rejected the call once again.

After pushing my books to the side, I laid back and reflected on how much my life had changed. For the most part, Jayceon was good to me. Nobody is perfect. I had to deal with Nae Nae, and him being in the streets, but I loved him! Sometimes deep down, when I searched my heart, I started thinking that love was making a damn fool out of me!

Jayceon had never been one to do things to swept me off my feet. Sometimes I wished he could be more understanding about how I feel. He usually brushed things to the side when I let him know something was bothering me. Like right now; why the fuck is this bitch calling my goddamn phone! And how in the hell does she keep getting my number?

It irked me to the core that Nae Nae still posed a threat to me. And Jayceon continues to act as if it's no big deal which makes things worse. I swear, if I didn't have nothing but love for him, I would've left his ass a while ago and let some other chick deal with this stress.

I received another call from the unknown number and this time I answered. "Hello!" I yelled.

"Aye, don't be yelling at me, bitch! Where my man at?"

I sat up after Nae Nae's question. Really? How boldfaced can one bitch get; calling my phone as if she pays the mothafuckin' bill.

"Well, clearly he ain't your man if you callin' my phone, inquiring about where he's at?" I replied to her and I twisted my neck as if she could see my head movements.

"The only reason I'm calling your stupid ass is because he's not answering his phone, so I thought he was with yo' dumb ass. But from the sound of it, he's not with you either." She chuckled at what she'd said, which only added to my anger.

"Look! I would appreciate if you would stop callin' my phone, OK? I don't know how you keep getting my number anyway." I was about to move the phone away from my ear when she started laughing hysterically.

"You know, for a college bitch, you sure are dumb! Bitch, Gucci still fucks me. What you think, he just quit my ass. Honey, I have been with Gucci way before he had these streets on lock. We have history, and it doesn't matter who he gets with, he always comes right back to me and his son. Besides, you think I'm just gon' let you or any other trick come in and reap the benefits of all the work I done put in with that man? You must've lost your mind. You gon' have to deal with me from now until I say you don't have to anymore. So, enjoy your little time you have with MY man, bitch!"

I listened quietly until Nae Nae ended the call, and I placed my phone back on the bed next to me. And once again, the tears formed! I blinked repeatedly and tried my best to prevent them from falling because what she'd said, made me feel some type of way.

Was this really what I signed up for when I got with Jayceon? To be hassled nonstop by a female who refused to let go of someone that claimed he didn't want shit to do with her? Should I even believe what she said to me? It could explain how she keeps getting my number. But then again, Jayceon would have to be dumb as fuck if he kept leaving his phone around where she could easily get it.

I confided in Matika about Nae Nae's phone calls once, and she said that if Nae Nae knew someone that works at my phone provider's company, they could easily pull up my name up and give her the information that she wanted!

As if Nae Nae's annoying ass hadn't been enough stress on me, Jayceon informed me that morning that he'd be heading to Venezuela for a few days. He claimed that he and his connect had teamed up with somebody named, Eduardo, and that Eduardo was about to make him a very rich man with the biggest shipment he'd ever had.

How much money does one person need? I'd seen Jayceon's bank statement numerous times, and his balance was ridiculous. It made me wonder why the fuck I was going to college, when clearly I needed to be pushing some serious dope!

Who was I kidding though? I couldn't sell dope if my life depended on it. So, it was back to pushing these books. I sighed and grabbed my books to begin studying again. I wasn't going to bother mentioning to Jayceon that Nae Nae had called because it wouldn't change a goddamn thing. All he'd do is brush it off and say that I'm being insecure as always.

The more I thought about it, the more I knew that my breaking point was near. On the plus side, Jayceon's birthday would be coming up soon, and I wanted to do something extremely nice for him. I just didn't know what, yet. I still had about a week to decide, though. In the meantime, back to pushing these books.

*****

I bit my nails and headed towards the front door of the classroom. Jayceon insisted on picking me up today, so I didn't attend school in my car. I hoped and prayed that I was successful in passing my exams because lord knows my mind was all over the place yesterday.

As I walked outside, my eyes searched for Jayceon's Range, but there was no sign of it. I hoped Jayceon remembered that he had to come get me. I sucked my teeth and opened my bag to get my phone and call him. He answered on the first ring.

"Jay, did you forget that you're supposed to pick me up from class today?" I asked in annoyance because he never missed a day of being in those damn streets, yet had the nerve to forget to pick my ass from class!

"Now, how would I ever forget to come get my baby? I'm looking at you."

"Huh?" Again, I scanned the line of cars parked in the front, but still didn't see his Range. And his Gucci Maybach would've been spotted a mile away. "Jay, I don't see you anywhere. Quit playing!"

I heard a horn blowing and followed the sound. I laid my eyes on a brand new, candy apple 2016 Porsche Cayenne. "What in the hell!" I removed the phone from my ear and walked toward the car where Jayceon was sitting behind the wheel, cheesing like crazy.

"Really Jay?" I said, shaking my head as he unlocked the doors for me to hop in.

"You like? I decided to get myself an early birthday present," Jayceon said as he pulled into the street.

I peeped the interior and couldn't deny that it was a nice vehicle. Everything smelled fresh and new.

"I'll be leaving in the morning for Venezuela, aight."

I pretended like I didn't hear what he'd just said by turning my head to look out my window because lord knows if I had replied to is his stupid ass, we would've ended up arguing. So, I choose the smartest thing to do which was to keep my mouth shut!

"Shaunie, don't you hear a nigga talking to you?" Jayceon asked in an irritated tone. He let out an annoyed sigh.

"I hear you," I said.

"I don't even know what your problem is right now? I told yo' ass that I'd be goin', didn't I? So, stop trippin'. You comin' over later? Your man needs some of that honey pussy before I go."

Just then, I turned and looked at him. *Is this nigga serious? Going to leave my ass, go to Venezuela, and on top of that is asking for some pussy! He must be crazy.*

"Nah, I'm on my period. You'll get when you come back, I guess." I turned my lying ass around to look out the window.

Sometimes I can't help the petty shit that comes out my mouth, but I swear on everything, Jayceon made me this way! Men have a way of changing women. It's either you change and become a better person, or fucking around with niggas like Jay that wrap their bullshit around a young impressionable, naïve mind like the one I had, they make you become a goddamn fucked up mess.

"Wait, weren't you on your period like two and a half weeks ago?" I felt him burning a hole through the side of my head as he asked. Jayceon made it his business to keep track of shit like that. He claimed that if I were fucking around on him, he'd know because my period would get thrown off its regular cycle.

"Yeah, but I think the stress of preparing for this exam caused it to come early or something."

He continued looking at me as if he didn't believe me, so I decided to change the topic. "What you wanna do for your birthday? You'll be back home in time, right?" I said as I looked at him.

He looked as if he was still thinking about me telling him that I was on my period, but the look disappeared as he answered. "I don't know, maybe go to a club and get turnt up or some shit."

I scrunched my face and rolled my eyes at his response. I definitely would not be taking him to a club because he'd probably fuck around and get kicked out the club on his damn birthday. "We'll see about that," I said to him, but I already had an idea of what I wanted to do for him. I just had to get a little help with the preparation from Jazmine.

"You know what would be a nice gift?" He said as he pulled onto my street.

"What's that?"

"If you'll finally move in with a nigga. Damn, how many times do I have to ask you? A nigga gettin' tired of asking." He parked the car in front of my house but kept the engine running. He looked at me and took my hand.

This isn't the first time that we'd had this conversation. Jayceon asked me this question a couple of times before. I honestly didn't think I was ready to live with Jay. Furthermore, I didn't think Jayceon was ready! If Nae Nae was tripping now, what the fuck would she do if she found out that we were living together? Not to mention the lonely ass nights I'd have to face with him gone all the damn time.

"Jay, you sure you're ready for us to live together? I mean, your baby momma is tripping all the time, and you always chasing them Benjamins. You probably won't ever be at home with me. I'll think about it while you're gone, OK?"

And I honestly was going to. *Maybe if we lived together, I could somehow convince him to not be in the streets so much.*

"Aight, well since I'm not getting no pussy, get out my damn car, man." Jayceon fell out laughing thinking that he was cute for his little statement.

I mushed his head as I opened the door.

"Hey, hold up. You won't be able to contact me when I'm over there, aight. I'll call you 7:30 every night, so make sure to be by your damn phone, Shaunie! Don't have me call and you don't pick up. You don't want them kinda' problems."

It irritated me that he said I wouldn't be able to call him if I needed to. I said nothing about it though. "Jayceon?" I said before I got out his new ride.

"Yeah babe."

"You love me?" I always wanted to be reassured that he did. I swear, it helped me sleep better at night.

"You know I do. Come here."

I leaned in, and he did the same. We met each other halfway. Our mouths connected, and I moaned softly as I savored the feel of his tongue invading my mouth. I swear on everything----I loved me some Jayceon more than the streets ever would! I kissed away all my doubts that Nae Nae had planted in my head. And I kissed away the fact that my man was going to leave me for a few days.

"Damn, you gon' make a nigga fuck around and run through that red light that you're on, Shaunie," Jayceon said after he pulled his lips away from mine. Then he laid his forehead against mine.

I suddenly felt bad for the lie that I'd told earlier, so I got out the car. "Call me as soon as you can when you get there, OK," I told him as I got out and closed the door behind me.

"Aight baby, I'll text you when I get home, aight."

I waved goodbye as he waited for me to get into the house. Then he drove off.

After helping the nurse with my mother who seemed to be in high spirits, I took a bath then lay in bed. Because it was so early, I couldn't get to sleep; it was only 8:00. I picked up my phone to check if Jayceon had texted to let me know that he'd gotten home. He hadn't.

This wasn't the first time that he'd done this, so I was just going to let it slide. But it was like something was telling me to pick up the phone and call him. So, I did. The phone rang repeatedly. I called over five times, but he never answered.

Growing up, I'd always heard my mother talk about a woman's intuition, and let's just say that mine was kicking the fuck out of me! I tried his number once again, and it rang out again until it went to voicemail.

Not being able to shake the feeling I was getting at the pit of my stomach, I got up and got dressed. I threw a pair of Nike sweatpants and a matching sweater on, then hurriedly found the nurse and told her that I'd be back in a few minutes. I grabbed my keys for my X5, hopped in, and made drove to Jayceon's house.

As I drove, I kept thinking that he may have just fallen asleep and wasn't hearing his phone ring. Or maybe he was upstairs, his phone downstairs, and I was tripping for no reason. That's until I arrived at his house and there was a Chevy Impala parked there; a car I'd never seen before. It was parked right next to his brand new Porsche.

I cautiously climbed out of my BMW then stood next to mystery car. I peered into the car and saw a car seat in the back. *I have no idea what type of car Nae Nae drives, but this better not be her shit parked up in his driveway!*

I took out my keys and walked toward the house. I unlocked the door then stepped inside.

CHAPTER 20

I started up the stairs and barely made two steps before I heard voices from upstairs. I paused as I saw two people emerge from the top of the stairs. Jayceon and Nae Nae took a while before they spotted me, and I swear Jayceon was acting like he was doing the mannequin challenge or some shit. That nigga didn't move at all when he made eye contact with me. Nae Nae on the other hand, had a devilish smile on her face.

"Thanks for everything, Gucci," Nae Nae said seductively as she smiled at me and made her way down the stairs. I took one final look at Jayceon before turning to walk back through the door.

"Shaunie! Yo, hold up, man." Jayceon reached me in record time as I was opening the door to get the hell out of there.

He grabbed for my arm, and I used all my strength to pull away from him.

"Don't you fuckin' touch me, Jayceon Clarke!" I spat, as I glowered at him. I reached once more for the door, but Jayceon refused to let me open it.

He put the palm of his hand flat against the door. "Man, calm the fuck down. She's just over here 'cause I asked her to come get a stash for my son so he'll be straight while I'm gone. Ain't nothing happened with me and her."

I looked at him and started to laugh like a mental patient. *Jayceon must think I'm stupid.* "Oh yeah? That's why the two of you were coming from your bedroom, right?"

I heard Nae Nae chuckle at what I'd said, and I cut my eyes at her. *If she so much as says one word to me . . .*

"Do you know how crazy you sound right now? We weren't coming from my bedroom, Shaunie. I went to get the money and she asked if she could use the bathroom real quick. I was coming downstairs because I realized I left my phone in my whip and was coming down to get it. That's it, I swear on my daddy nothin' happened."

I looked at Jayceon with a blank expression because honestly, I was so over it. "Have a good night, Jayceon," I said quietly as I turned once again to leave. Only God knew the way my heart was breaking into about a million pieces.

"Bye, bitch," I heard Nae Nae say as I turned the doorknob.

Now, remember when I said that I'd reached my breaking point? Well, that was my word.

I turned around, walked past Jayceon, raised my hand, and slapped Nae Nae like a hoe that had come up short on paying her pimp. The sound of that slap echoed throughout the entire house.

Nae Nae lunged for me, but I was ready for her ass and slapped her again. Jayceon grabbed a hold of her as she kicked and screamed, and dragged her to the front door.

"Man, Nae Nae, get the fuck out. Let me deal with my girl. I gave you the money for my son. You gotta' bounce!" Jayceon opened the door and practically threw Nae Nae out the door.

"Fuck you, Gucci!" she screamed at him just before he closed the door in her face.

He moved towards me, but I held out my hand for him to stop. "Jayceon, I don't even care anymore. I'm sick of this shit. I've been calling you for the past hour only to come here to see you got Nae Nae up in your crib. She can have your sorry, lying ass. I'm good!" With those words, I brushed past him.

He grabbed my hand, and in one swift movement, he had me pinned against the front door. "Fuck me, Shaunie? Talking all that shit. You think I want Nae Nae? I done told you so many times, she's just the mother of my son. When you gon' get that through your thick mothafuckin' head, Shauntel? I told you I forgot my phone in the Porsche."

I was trying my best not to look him in his eyes by turning my head away, but he kept putting his hand under my chin which forced me to look at him.

"You good? Huh, Shauntel? You good. Think you just gonna' walk out that door and what? Never come back? You fuckin' crazy? I know I may not be one of those sensitive ass type of niggas you may want me to be, Fuck all that. I'm from the streets. But I fuckin' love you. Nae Nae just hating on the fact that I don't want her stupid ass!"

All the while he screamed at me with his face inches from mine, I did what Shauntel Harris does best----cry. Those tears were running down my cheeks hotter than a mothafucka. They felt like they were burning the hell out of my face.

"Jayceon, I can't do this anymore. Just let me go, please!" I said in between sobs. I was tired of all the constant fighting and bickering about the same shit over and over. Shit had me exhausted.

"Hell naw, I'm not letting you go a goddamn place. Look at me baby. Look at me." He placed his hands on the sides of my face and forced my head to turn toward him. He then kissed my tears away as they streamed down my face. His kisses moved to the side of my neck and trailed to between my breasts.

My tears stopped, and my breaths were now becoming short gasps.

Even though I loved the feel of his mouth on me, I started pushing him off . . . or was I pulling him into me?

I thought that he'd forgotten I had lied and said that I was on my period because his hands settled between my thighs. Jayceon looked up at me with a surprised look on his face, and I realized that I'd been caught in my own lie!

"Well, aren't we a little liar. Let me show you what happens to naughty girls who lie."

My back was still pinned against the wall as Jayceon got on his knees and roughly pulled my sweatpants off and my panties right along with them. He hooked my right leg onto his shoulder and spread my pussy open with his hands. With one fast flick of his tongue, he licked furiously at my clit, which caused me to cry out.

Jayceon ate my pussy as if he was mad at it. His licks were fast and hard. He rolled his tongue over and over in circles and sucked every last drop of my sweet, sticky wetness that seeped out of me. I shoved my hand into the back of his head as I pushed my pelvis forward into his face.

"I swear, Shaunie, you got the sweetest, fattest, and prettiest pussy in the whole world," Jayceon said in between licks.

Looking down at him and seeing the way he feasted on me, brought me to an orgasm that had me crying. Those fucking tears would not stop rolling down my face. This man right here was going to be the death of me.

After licking up every last drop of my juices, Jayceon got up. He took my leg off his shoulder, put his hand on the back of my knee, and placed the tip of his dick at my opening. He stopped to kiss me for a brief second, then rammed his dick into me with such force that I cried out into his mouth. Jayceon placed his hand under my left knee and lifted me. I was now suspended in the air as he fucked me hard up against the door, causing it to bang repeatedly.

"Tell me you love me baby," Jayceon said as he sucked my ear lobe.

"Aaahhh . . . I love you Jay . . . I love you baby." I tried my best to get those words pass my lips. *Good lord, the way he's smashing my pussy, I'm gonna be sore for the entire time he's gone!*

"Fuuuccckkk, Shauntel. You gon' make me buss a nut too quick, man . . .shit!" Jayceon said as he started sucking on my neck hard. Then he slammed me against the door.

My hands were wrapped tightly against his neck, and my eyes

were shut as I breathlessly enjoyed the feel of Jayceon's dick hitting all the right spots.

As I said before----we fought, then we fucked. I was a sucker for his dick!

CHAPTER 21

I wiggled in my seat as I sat in class the next day. My pussy felt as if I'd sat on an ant's nest!

I spent the night at Jayceon's. We never made it to his bedroom. We slept wrapped up on his sofa until he got up to leave for his flight to Venezuela. He took me home in my car, and Maliq picked him up from there. I was hoping that his connect came to get him so that I could see exactly what a dirty cop looked like!

Jayceon had promised that he would call to let me know when he landed, which should've been more than two hours ago. As I got ready to leave school for the day, I checked my phone once more; still, nothing from Jayceon.

I let out a sigh as I gathered my belongings in preparation to call it a day. I was pretty damn exhausted and just wanted to get home. After I went outside, I disarmed the alarm to Jayceon's candy apple red Porsche! Yup, Jayceon gave me the keys after dropping me off at home. I was more than excited to drive back over there to leave my X5 and drive away in his Porsche!

After pulling out of the parking lot at school, a thought hit me; I hadn't seen Cocoa in ages. So, I decided to pay her a visit at the coffee shop where I used to work. The coffee shop was just a few minutes away from the college. With little traffic, I made it in under ten minutes.

Cocoa was taking a customer's order when I walked in, so I stood to the side and waited. While waiting, I took a good look at the girl that had replaced me. *She seems pleasant enough,* I thought as she gave the customers their orders with a smile.

"Hey, Cocoa," I said as I walked up to her after she was through with the last customer.

She looked at me and gave a faint smile. "Hey, Shauntel. What brings you all the way over here?" she asked sarcastically.

"Girl, quit playing and give me a hug," I said as I stretched over the counter to give Cocoa a quick embrace.

"And how is life with Gucci Boss?" Cocoa asked and smiled faintly.

I rolled my eyes in an exaggerated way.

"Girl, it has its ups and downs. You know how it go," I said with a wave of my hand to dismiss her question.

Cocoa asked her coworker to cover for her so that we could catch up. While we chatted it up, Cocoa brought something to my attention. "Oh! By the way, your friend comes in sometimes and asks for you every time!"

That caught my attention, and I looked at her with puzzled expression on my face.

"Who's that, Cocoa?"

"Well, I can't recall his name but he seemed sweet on you. Gucci caught you and him chatting it up one time."

As Cocoa words sank in, I realized who she was speaking about. "You mean, Chase!" I said in a near whisper.

"Yeah, that's his name."

I was in shock because I would sometimes wonder about Chase; about where he'd been, what he was up to, if he was studying law, or if he still acted as a substitute teacher. I was happy that I could finally get some sort of message across to him.

"Look, Cocoa, next time you see him, can you please give him my number? I would like to catch up and see how he's been doing," I said as I wrote my name and number down.

"Naw, no need for all that," Cocoa said abruptly, which made me stop and look up at her.

"He just walked in, so you can tell him yourself."

Is Cocoa joking right now? My back was to the door, so I wouldn't have been able to see anyone who walked in. I was almost too scared to turn around and see if it was really him.

Without warning, I saw Cocoa look behind me and smile as she rose from her seat and walked away.

In her place now, sat Chase! I looked at him as if I was in a dream and smiled at him because I was truly happy to see him. Not to mention, Chase looked as fine as ever in a white Lacoste button up, slim-fit black Levi's, along with a pair of black Chuck Taylor's. He even smelled like something to eat. Smiling back at me, he said, "Hello, Shauntel."

CHAPTER 22

"*Hey*, Chase, it's been a while, huh?" I said as we kept smiling at each other.

Chase interlocked his fingers as he looked at me. It was like I was seeing him for the first time, and I liked what I was seeing! Chase looked like he'd been hitting up the gym as his muscles appeared a little bigger. He also had some of facial hair that was forming a beard.

"It's been way too long, Shauntel. I come up in here every so often, just hoping I'll get too see you; hoping that you'll stop by to check in on your friend. Why you stop calling me? I felt really bad about our last conversation and what I said. I want to say that I'm sorry for that."

Chase sounded so sincere that I forgave him instantly. He put my hands in his and gently caressed my knuckles with his fingertips.

"Chase, I should be the one saying sorry. I may have overreacted. So, I'm sorry. But you know what, let's forget about it. Tell me what you've you been up to? Are you practicing law yet?" I wanted him to tell me everything that had happened in his life since the last time we'd spoken. I didn't want him to leave out a single detail.

"Nah, I'm not practicing law. Well, not really."

Damn, can he be anymore vague? I watched the way he avoided

eye contact when he said that shit, too. Almost as if he didn't really want to answer the question. As I was about to ask him what was up with him avoiding my question, he spoke up.

"Forget all that for now. Tell me how college is going?"

Chase and I sat there for damn near over an hour catching up on the status of my classes, my mother's health, and he even asked me about my relationship with Jayceon.

"So, how's the boyfriend that almost killed my ass?" Chase asked as he put his hand on the back of his head and rubbed gently.

I began to feel bad because I remembered him saying that he' had to get stitches where he was hit in the head with Jayceon's gun butt.

"He's fine. He went out of the country for a few days." I looked down at our hands which were still interlocked, and subtly pulled away because I had no business holding his hand and shit as if we were lovers having coffee.

"Wow, he's not in the country and he left you behind. He must be confident than a mothafucka."

I laughed at the unexpected use of his curse word. It was actually the first time that I'd ever heard him curse.

"Why you laugh?"

"'Cause, I've never heard you curse before. It was just strange, I guess."

He smiled, and I noticed that the corners of his eyes crinkled when he did.

What the hell is my problem? Acting like some lovesick teenager.

Get it together, Shauntel! I scolded myself in my head.

"Man, I cuss like I ain't got no damn sense most of the time. You just haven't been around me that much to get to know the real me."

He looked into my eyes as he spoke, and like a damn fool, I felt myself blush. My cheeks got warm, and I looked away nervously.

"Why you lookin' away and playin' all shy and shit. Look at me, Shauntel."

I turned my eyes back to him.

"Do you know how much I like you? How much I wish that you could be mine? I used to look at you walk from class and wish that I could get to know you better. Until one day, I finally said fuck it and got the courage to step to you. Let me take you out sometime. Besides, you owe me; I was supposed to take you out for your birthday, remember?"

I listened attentively because what he was saying came as a shock. I never thought that he'd felt that way about me. But I'll be damned if Jayceon murdered my ass for acting like a common slut out in these streets while he's gone.

"Look, Chase, you know how my man gets down. I'm not even trying to get on his bad side for both of our sakes."

Chase looked at me and sucked his teeth. He shook his head, huffed, and sounded annoyed all of a sudden. "Man, Shaunie. No disrespect, but why you like him? Don't you see he's all wrong for you? Keep fucking with that nigga and he gone end up dead or in prison. You ready for that?" Chase looked me up and down while awaiting a reply.

He was going to have to wait for an answer though because I had thought about this so many times that it made head hurt. I had thought that I would be enough for Jayceon and that he would eventually change his ways, but I was wrong.

"Let's not go there, alright. Look, I gotta' go. I need to be home by 7:00." I started to gather my belongings that were laid out on the table. I really didn't want to get into an argument with Chase; not after finally meeting up with him after all these months.

"Nah, hold up. You not about to go this time without giving me your number, Shauntel. I can't risk never being able to get in contact with you again." He fished his phone out of his pocket, unlocked it and stood up.

I was unsure if it would be a wise thing to give him my number. I started chewing on my lower lip as I studied him. "OK, but you have to promise that when he gets back, you won't contact me. Instead, you'll wait for me to contact you." I didn't want to risk my phone going off in Jayceon's presence. He'd immediately get suspicious because I rarely get calls.

Chase tilted his head to the side and looked at me as if he was mad that I had even suggested such terms. "You buggin', Shauntel, for real. But cool, I'll play along . . . for now that is!"

I took Chase's phone from his grasp, quickly logged my number, then handed his phone back to him. He looked down at the screen and smiled like he was so happy to have my number stored in his phone.

"Let me walk out with you real quick." He took my hand as he led me out of the shop.

I waved goodbye to Cocoa who wagged her finger at me as if she'd caught me doing something naughty. I waved her off.

"I'm parked over here," I told Chase as I pointed to Jayceon's Porsche.

Chase let go of my hand and he put his hand over his mouth as he gave and exaggerated howl. "Say word! Homeboy got you stomping with the big dogs, huh?" Chase walked around the car like he had never seen a damn Porsche before.

"Boy, quit playing. It's just a car, and technically it's not mine." I laughed as I unlocked the door and hopped in.

Chase came over to the driver's side and leaned against the door as I started the ignition. "You'll think about what I said right? Let me take you out sometime, and don't go making any excuses either. If you don't wish to be seen in public with me, I'll take you to my place and make you dinner. Damn, let a nigga show you a good ass time!"

I laughed at what he'd said, and we stared at each other for a few seconds. For the first time since being involved with Jayceon, I felt my pussy react to someone other than him. My clit was pulsing and aching in a sweet, wonderful way in response to how Chase was looking at me at that moment. I wiggled in my seat a little in hopes of easing the way my body was reacting to him.

"Ok, we'll see, aight. Now move before I run your ass over with my Porsche."

We laughed in unison as he stepped back and allowed me to back out. I waved him goodbye and drove to the highway. I tried my best to concentrate on the road, but my thoughts were racing as I thought about finally seeing Chase again after more than six months.

I didn't think that it would be wise to encourage him. I knew going to dinner with him would not be smart by the way my body reacted to him and the fact that all he did was look at my ass. I'd fuck around and end up a dead bitch if Jayceon found out that I even spoke to Chase again!

Right then, I decided to stay the hell away from Chase Evans. Fucking around with his ass was just going to land me in a whole heap of trouble that I can do without!

CHAPTER 23

"*Hey* baby what's your sexy self up to?" It was exactly 7:30, and just like he promised, Jayceon called. I was lying in bed having just got out the shower after helping the nurse see about my mother, when my phone rang. Jayceon's voice vibrated in my ear and sounded so sexy.

"I just got out the shower and finished checking on my mom. How's everything going over there." I played with my hair as I waited for his reply.

"I'm gonna be one rich mothafucka when I get back. How's my girl doin'? And I don't mean your ass."

My hand stilled in my hair. I was confused at his question. "What you mean, you don't mean me? So, who the fuck do you mean then, Jay!" After waiting to hear from his ass all day, he had the nerve to ask about some random trick.

Jayceon started laughing. "Man, chill out, Shaunie, damn. I just meant your pussy. You my girl, but that's my baby right there for real."

I sucked my teeth, smiled, and shook my head at his silly ass. He was about to get cursed the hell out for saying some mess like that. "Jay, don't play with me like that. You know I don't like playing games."

"You miss me, baby? I can't wait to see your ass when I get home."

I smiled shyly. What woman didn't want to hear that her man missed her. "You know I miss you. When you coming home? Please don't say that you won't be back in time for your birthday," I said and pouted as if he could see me. I'd already planned what I was going to do for him, and I didn't want my planning to go to waste.

"I'll probably be here for the next two days. So I'll be back in time for my birthday. What you got planned for a nigga?" I could tell he was smiling when he asked that question and I smiled in response.

"Mind your damn business, Jay. Just bring your goofy ass home."

"Yeah, as soon as I get back I'm gon' put this goofy dick up inside your sweet pussy!"

I laughed and shook my head.

Jayceon and I spoke for almost forty-five minutes, he kept telling me how much he missed me and I kept telling him to hurry home.

"Aight, baby, I gotta go. Tell a nigga you love him."

I was sad that we were about to end our call. I hadn't thought that I would missed his ass so much since we argued liked cats and dogs most of the time.

"I miss you baby, hurry up and get back home. We miss you. And by "we", I mean me and my pussy," I said as I laughed.

Jayceon chuckled in response. "Aight, baby. I love you, too. Call you the same time tomorrow."

We said our final goodbyes as he disconnected our call. I laid there for a few minutes reminiscing about Jayceon. I couldn't even front, Chase popped into my head so many times that I was mad at myself. I forced myself to go to sleep.

The next morning, my phone woke me up. I didn't have class today, so I decided to sleep a little late. Something I rarely do. Without looking at the screen, I grabbed the phone from under my pillow and answered it sleepily.

"Don't tell me you still asleep?" a sexy, deep voice said into my ear.

I began rubbing my eyes vigorously as I pulled the phone away from my ear and looked at the screen. It was Chase. What in the hell? Looking at the time on my screen, I saw that it was just after 9:00.

"Hey Chase, what's up?" I sat up as I tried futilely to brush strands of hair from my face. I hated when I forgot to put my stocking cap on because I would wake up with my hair looking like the Bride of Frankenstein.

"Nothing, was hoping I'd get to see you today. What you think. Gonna' make time for me? I know you said that you didn't have to go class today."

Shit! I cannot be around this man. That wouldn't be a good idea. But my body is betraying the hell out of me by responding to Chase the way that it is. "Uuummm, I'm not sure. I have some last-minute planning to do for Jayceon's birthday which is coming up. I may not have much time."

At least that wasn't a complete lie. I did plan to pick up Jayceon's sister, Jazmine, and hit up the mall so that we could buy a few things for his surprise birthday party that I'd planned to have at his mom's house. That wouldn't take long, but Chase didn't have to know all that!

"Really, Shauntel? Are you gonna' make me beg? C'mon man. Besides, you owe me, remember?"

I exhaled softly. I said a quick prayer asking God to give me the strength to not let my body be loose. "OK, Chase. When I get back from shopping, I'll give you a call, aight?"

I closed my eyes and exhaled silently. As I removed the phone from my ear, I heard him say something, so I quickly put it up to my ear again.

"I have one small request, OK? Don't get mad."

My interest was piqued in regard to what he was about to say, so I sat in silence and waited to hear his request.

"You don't need all that extra. I mean, all the makeup and weave. You don't need that. Gimme' the old makeup and weave-free Shauntel back!"

Unconsciously, I ran my fingers through my tangled hair. I knew I didn't need it, but Jayceon would drop me off every two weeks to get it done, and he didn't mind me getting extensions. He also introduced me to wearing makeup. I had absolutely no problem with leaving them out my daily routine to be honest.

"Well, aren't we bossy. But OK, I'll see what I can do," I said to Chase as I got out of bed.

"Well that's what's up! I'll see you later."

I creased my eyebrows as I disconnected the call. I'd swear Chase was a street nigga when I listened to him speak sometimes. But being the only son of a high-ranking police officer would've gotten his ass beat if he thought about being in the streets. I started stripping my clothes off and getting prepared for the day ahead.

*****

"Damn, Jazmine, will you make up your fuckin' mind already!" Me and Jazmine had been in the mall for damn near three hours, and she still couldn't chose a gift for her brother, I should've just left her ass at her mom's house.

"I don't know what to get him, Shaunie." Jazmine whined like a damn three-year-old.

We'd been to about five different stores at Lenox Square Mall, and she was still confused. I was getting frustrated as hell with her little ass.

"Jazmine, you're irritating the hell out of me. Let's go to the Cartier store so I can buy my gift for Jay." I grabbed hold of her hand and walked her in the direction of the store.

A couple weeks before, when I was at the mall with Matika, I saw this insane watch that I knew Jayceon would love. It was a Ballon Bleu De Cartier eighteen carat white gold watch with over one hundred diamonds in the face. I'd been able to save enough over the past few months with money that Jayceon had given me plus money I'd saved while working at the coffee shop. This watch was something serious. It was expensive as hell.

"Hi, can you give me this watch right here," I said as I pointed it out to the white sales clerk. She was a blonde, uptight looking bitch who looked me over like I couldn't afford it. Obviously, she'd never seen the movie "Pretty Woman". If she had then maybe she would've learned to never to judge a book by its cover.

"That watch is a very expensive piece." She looked me up and down and turned her nose up at me.

Before I got a chance to respond, Jazmine was all up in her face. "Aye, did she ask you for the price? She said she wanted to buy the watch. Now hurry your lil' stuck up ass up and give it to her!"

This Jasmine! If she didn't calm her hostile ass down, she was going to fuck around and have these white people kick our asses out their damn store before I could get Jay's gift.

"My apologies, but my little sister suffers from Tourette's! She just blurts shit out without knowing what she's doing. Can I have the watch, please?"

That white chick looked pissed the hell off as she opened the glass case and grabbed the watch. Jazmine was standing there snickering as she watched how irritated the sales clerk was. I cut my eyes at her, and she quieted.

After pulling out my card and paying for my purchase, the sales clerk didn't make any form of eye contact as she handed the gift box over to me. Jazmine and I left the store, and as soon as we walked out, she burst out laughing.

"The nerve of your ass to tell that stuck up bitch that I got Tourette's!" She was laughing so hard that tears were rolling down her face.

I stood over her as she bent over and held her stomach while laughing her ass off. Before long, I couldn't help but laugh myself.

"Girl, c'mon. Let's go to the Louis Vuitton store. And we're not leaving until you get him something with yo' crazy ass. I swear you have no chill just like your damn brother." Taking her hand, I led her in the direction of the store.

She was finally able to stop laughing, and wiped the tears off her face.

I got home around 5:00. Jazmine had me out all day, running from one place to the next. Thank God that I'd worn a comfortable pair of low cut Chuck Taylors, or I would've dropped her ass back at her house a long time ago. I walked into my mom's room, and she was sitting up in bed as the nurse fed her.

She smiled faintly as I walked in. "Hey, baby," she said softly.

I swear my heart pulled into my chest. My mother looked so frail. She wasn't wearing her scarf on her head, and almost all of her hair was gone.

I walked over and took the spoon away from the nurse. "It's Ok, take a break. I'll feed her." I smiled at the nurse.

She was such a pleasant lady that always wore a smile on her heart-shaped face. She nodded and let go of the spoon. As she got up to leave, she gently patted my mother on her hand and left the room.

"How are you feeling today, Mom?" I asked as I spoon-fed her what looked like oatmeal.

She opened her mouth slowly as I gently placed the spoon in her mouth. "I'm good, baby. How are you doing and how is school? You're making sure to keep those good grades you're used to getting, I hope." She spoke so softly that I had to bend forward so that I could hear her.

"Of course, I am. You know I wouldn't let you down. I just wish you could get better so that you could be there for my graduation." Even though those words passed my lips, I knew it wouldn't be possible for my mother to attend. She was just too sick. *Fuck cancer,* I thought as I felt my eyes brim with tears. *Why did I have to lose both parents? It just wasn't fair.* I shook my head at my thoughts.

"Look at me, Shaunie."

I looked into her warm, gentle eyes and forced a smile.

"I want you to know that no matter what, I love you so much and I'm proud to say that you're my daughter. I know that your father was very proud of you also. Don't give up on your dreams and know that no matter where you are, or how lost and alone you may feel at times, I will always be with you in your heart. I may not approve of the choice that you made to be with Jayceon, but I think he really does care about you. He just has his priorities mixed up. I want you to take comfort in knowing that I'm glad you're my daughter and that I will always love you, my Shaunie baby."

I put the bowl of oatmeal down on the nightstand and hugged my mother like I'd never hugged her before. My heart swelled up in my chest, and even though I thought I would cry, I didn't. We hugged and comforted each other for a couple minutes, then I filled her in on Jayceon's birthday celebration and continued feeding her.

After taking care of my mother, I went into my room, put away Jay's gift, and stripped out of my white slim jeans and Prada top. I sat on the bed in my matching bra and underwear set from Victoria's Secret then started taking my shoes off when my phone rang. I picked it up and froze as Chase's name popped up on the screen. I took a deep breath then answered the call.

"Hey, Chase. I was just about to call you." Sometimes my mouth moved faster than my brain because that was a damn lie! I'd forgotten all about Chase after running around with Jazmine all day.

"Damn, Shauntel. I thought you'd forgot all about me. What time should I come get you?"

I forgot about taking my other shoe off and used my hand to rub my temples instead. I'd be damned if I go anywhere with Chase and risk being alone with him. I didn't trust myself around him. But somehow, I felt as if I owed it to him. When we were about to leave the coffee shop, I saw the scar on the back of his head and felt guilty as sin.

"Give me directions to where you live, and I'll be over in the next hour or so," I replied as I shook my head. I knew this was something that I shouldn't be doing, but I'd make sure this was the first and last time that I'd be making a risky decision like this one where Chase was concerned.

After getting directions, I took my shoe off and stepped into the shower. I was about to make my way over to Chase's house.

CHAPTER 24

$\mathcal{I}$ made it to Chase's house about forty-five minutes after five. He lived in a fairly upscale part of Atlanta at a newly-built apartment complex. I parked my X5 in a visitor's spot on the side of the apartment. I took out my phone and dialed Chase to let him know that I was outside. I waited a couple of seconds, then Chase came out to meet me. Let me say this----I was prepared to jump right back into my car and get the hell out of there!

Chase strolled up to me wearing a plain V-neck t-shirt and a pair of grey sweat pants with all his meat swinging from left to right like nobody's business! I had to force myself to look away, but not before Chase caught me gawking at his package and gave me a cocky ass smile.

"Hey, Shauntel," he greeted me with a smile and hug.

"Hey, Chase," I replied nervously then cleared my throat as I followed his lead inside the apartment.

Chase lived on the second floor in a beautiful spacious apartment. It was decorated very masculinely in dark colors of black and chocolate brown. He had a black leather sectional in front of a huge flat screen TV. His walls were adorned with pictures of who I assumed was his family.

"Have a seat and relax. I was just finishing up cooking dinner."

I took a seat and looked as he made his way over to the kitchen where the scent of cooking food filled my nostrils. And I must say, it smelled wonderful. Who would've thought that Chase could throw down like Bobby Flay!

"What are you making?" I asked loud enough so that he could hear my question while he stirred something by the stove.

"Fettucine pasta with jumbo shrimp and fresh salad. Hope you're not allergic to seafood 'cause that would suck!"

I laughed softly because you would think that he would've asked that before he started cooking. "Well, lucky for you, I'm not."

About fifteen minutes after we'd started eating, Chase put on the movie, "Friday" with Ice Cube and Chris Tucker. I ate and laughed my head off at a movie I'd seen so many times. I sat Indian style and had finally begun to feel comfortable and enjoy myself. I even caught Chase staring at me a couple of times, but paid him no mind.

I even asked him again about his job, and for the second time, he brushed it off without really answering. I was beginning to think he was a stripper or some shit.

"I'm glad you didn't wear much make up. Never mind that you still got the weave in. That's cool." Chase brushed his hand against my cheek as he spoke, and I surprised myself when I didn't pull away.

I turned and looked at him as he sat next to me on the sofa. I had purposely not worn any makeup because, quite frankly, I didn't really like it too much. I wanted to take my extensions out but I didn't have enough time.

"Thanks," was all I managed to reply as he kept stroking my cheek.

And once again, my body started to betray me! My breath got caught in my throat, my nipples hardened against the short denim dress that I wore, and between my legs began to ache. Before I could try to stop Chase, he stopped on his own.

He grabbed our plates and he headed to the kitchen to place them in the sink. I used this opportunity to look at the photos that were hung on the wall because I needed something to distract me. I stood and looked at the photos one by one. I came across one with a slightly younger Chase and a man dressed in a police uniform. There was something awfully familiar about this man. I stared at the picture, then it hit me! This was the officer that Jayceon was speaking to on the day that his little brother, Jahvon, got arrested. What a small world.

Maybe that's why I found him to be so good looking the day I saw him at the station. Chase and his father looked so much alike. I don't know how it wasn't obvious to me that day. I decided not to mention to Chase that I'd seen his father because then I would have to explain where I saw him. And I didn't feel like getting into all of that.

"Hey, Chase, is this your dad?" I asked. As I turned around, I was surprised to see that Chase was standing right behind me. *How long had he been there?*

As he moved beside me, he replied, "Yeah, that's my old man. He never gave up on me. Even when I was out there trying to be a dope boy at a young age, he made sure to kept my ass in check! So, I ended up doing the right thing and stayed my ass in school. I'm really grateful to him for leading me in the right direction."

I don't know when he got so close to me that I was able to feel his breath on the side of my neck. *OK! This just won't do.* I turned around on my heel a little too fast, deciding that it would be better if I just left, when my clumsy ass twisted my ankle and fell flat on my ass!

"Oh, shit! Shauntel, are you OK?" Chase asked as he bent down to help me on my feet.

As soon as I applied pressure to my right foot, I screamed out in pain and sat back down on the floor. Before I'd realized what he was doing, Chase picked me up in his arms, walked to the sofa, and laid me down. He sat on the floor by my feet, took my sandals off, and examined my ankle with a worried expression on his face. I felt a little embarrassed as I winced in pain while he attempted to move my ankle in a circular motion.

"It's definitely sprained. Let me grab some ice for you."

I watched as Chase got up and headed to the kitchen once more. I laid my clumsy ass there and looked at my foot that was now swollen.

Chase came back with a Ziploc bag that had a few blocks of ice in it. He put it against my foot. He would stop every so often and massage my ankle gently, then replace his hands with the ice pack.

At some point during his nursing technique, I closed my eyes and let myself enjoy the feel his hands as he gently massaged my ankle. A small moan passed my lips without me meaning for it to happen.

"Do you love him, Shauntel?" Chase's voice brought me out of the daze I was in.

I looked down at him as he continued rubbing my ankle. *Huh? When did my dress reach that high up on my thigh, almost exposing my underwear?* I adjusted it and brought it down further on my thigh.

"What do you mean? If I love Jayceon?" I inquired.

"Yeah, him. Do you love him? Does he you make feel good? Instead of making love to your body, does he also make love to your mind? Does he only make your pussy wet and not your eyes? Does he tell you how beautiful you are without you needing all that fake shit on your face and in your hair? Tell me, Shauntel."

I listened to every word he said as he held my gaze. His hand moved from my ankle and was now rubbing on my calves, but his eyes never left mine.

I was unable to say anything because the only thing I could answer yes to was that I did love Jayceon, I truly did. I also knew that our relationship would be so much better if he could see that I loved him more than the streets, and if he could somehow put Nae Nae's annoying ass in check! I also understood that no relationship was perfect and there had to be compromise, but I just wished Jayceon could be a little bit more understanding to my feelings. However, I would never mention these things to Chase!

"Yes, Chase, I do love him. We may not have the perfect relationship, but I love him." I answered honestly. I saw Chase's jaw tighten as if my response angered him. Well, what the hell did he ask the question for if he didn't want an honest reply?

"Just give me this one time, to show you just how much I really care about you. I sometimes wish I would've let you know how I felt about you. To me, you deserve so much better. Just let me show you, Shauntel."

What in the hell was Chase asking of me? I couldn't allow him to have sex with me. That would be crazy. Not to mention that both Chase and I would make the 7:00 news if Jayceon ever found out.

"Look, I know you may feel some type of way toward me, but I can't have sex with you, Chase. I think it's time I leave. Thanks for dinner." I started sitting and tried not to move my injured ankle too quickly when Chase stopped me by putting his hand on my stomach.

"Yo, wait. Hold up. I never said I was going to have sex with you. Even though I saw the way you were checking out a niggas dick earlier." He chuckled softly as I bent my head in shame. "Nah look, I can show you how I can make your body buss' without a nigga even touching you or putting my mouth on you. But if at any time you want to feel my dick or my tongue on you, all you have to do is ask, and I'll happily oblige," Chase said as he licked his lips.

Chase was definitely a mix of a hood nigga and a white-collar nigga. One minute he spoke like a professor; next he was talking like one of those niggas on the block.

"I don't even know what you mean or what you plan to do, but it still sounds like something that I should not be doing." I attempted for a second time to rise from his sofa because, lord knows, I was physically attracted to this man. And it was not a good idea to be this close to him and doing something that I should not do!

"Let me show you. I promise, I won't touch you . . . much." As he spoke, his hands rubbed my legs and slowly crept up my inner thighs.

I swear on my daddy, I wanted that man to stop, but somehow my legs opened on their own, and I watched as Chase's hands made their way to my panties and started pulling them down.

"No, Chase. Stop. I shouldn't be doing this." I brushed his hand away from roaming any further.

He stared at me for a brief moment and stilled his hand. "Relax for me, Shaunie, I promise, you'll like it. Just relax," He said as he reassured me with the sweetest smile, which caused me to relax.

"Raise your hips for me, baby," Chase said softly and looked at me with so much lust in his eyes that I shamelessly did as I was told. He laid my panties on the floor next to where he sat and opened my legs a little more. Then he rocked forward and brought his mouth toward my wet, waiting pussy.

I tried to close them immediately. "Hold up, you said you weren't about to put your mouth on me," I said, a little confused.

"I'm not. Just relax and trust me, OK?" As he moved forward again, he made sure to hold my injured foot up with his grip under my knee. At the same time, he bent my other leg and held it open by holding it on my upper thigh. He moved into me again, and with his face directly in front of my pussy, he did something that I thought was weird at first. He started to blow air on my pussy!

I mean, what the fuck. Who does shit like that? But the more he did it, the more it started to feel so good. The way he moved his head in a circular motion, then back and forth against my clit, had me grinding my hips into the seat and moaning out loud before I knew it. I would've never in my wildest dreams thought that some random shit like this could ever feel this good.

I placed my hand on the back of his head and pushed his face into me because I wanted to feel his mouth on me. But he was resisted, and

I let out a frustrated cry.

"What you want, Shauntel? Tell Mr. Evans what you want," Chase said as he kissed inside my thigh.

He looked at me with sex in his eyes and made me moan again because his mouth was so close to where I wanted it to be.

"Please, please, Chase," I begged as I looked at him with my hand still on the back of his head. I pushed his head toward my pussy which was hurting because it was so aroused.

But he still resisted. "You need to tell me what you want, Shauntel. That's the only way you gonna' get it. I want to hear you beg for my tongue. Then I want to hear beg you for me to bury this dick in your stomach. Go ahead."

This nigga right here with his cocky ass! He put his mouth at a spot on the side of my pussy lips, bit it gently, then flicked his tongue on the same spot.

"Shit, Chase! Please, please eat my pussy. I'm begging you to."

No more words were needed as Chase dived right in. Using only the tip of his tongue, he flicked on my clit over and over again in quick movements. I looked down at him to see that his head was moving like one of those bobble head dolls; back and forth. I kept lifting my hips up towards his mouth as if I couldn't get enough because on the real, Chase had a thunder tongue.

Putting my clit between his lips, he sucked, let it pop out his mouth, then sucked again. He moved his mouth away from me and let a long trail of saliva drop from the off the tip off his tongue to my clit then slowly licked it off. Oh, my God! That sight alone had my stomach knotting for the orgasm I was about to have.

I took the back of his head again and shoved it into me. I cried out his name repeatedly as my orgasm rocked my body and caused me to shudder violently. I licked my lips because my mouth felt dry suddenly. In an attempt to come down from my high, I placed my hands over my face and closed my eyes. I was now left with the feeling of thinking less of myself. All I came to do was chill with Chase for a few minutes, not have him with his face buried in my pussy like some slut!

I groaned loudly and felt completely embarrassed and horrified. *What would Jayceon do if he found out what I did? Shit, Jayceon! What was the fucking time?* No sooner than the thought crossed my mind, my phone began ringing.

I pushed Chase to the side, careful not to hurt my sprained ankle, and proceeded to sit up. I pulled my phone out my purse, and sure enough it was Jayceon. My mind was a blur as I thought about whether I should answer it or not. Then I decided not to. If Jayceon decided that he wanted to face time, then what? I couldn't risk it. I took my time as I got up and headed for the front door.

"Shauntel, hold up, man. What's wrong with you?"

Still overcome with embarrassment, I couldn't even bring myself to look at Chase in his eyes. So, I averted my eyes and looked at my feet.

"Man, why are you staring at your feet? Look at me, Shauntel."

I still kept my head down. Chase took his hand, placed it under my chin, and forced my head up.

"So, what, are you embarrassed or some shit?"

I nodded. If there were a word bigger than embarrassed that would've been exactly how I felt right then. What was Chase supposed to think about me now; acting like some thot that can't keep her legs closed.

"So, you think I'm gonna' judge you or something, Shauntel? I've wanted you since the very first day I saw you, and I wanted this so bad. I will never judge or look at you any less. I really do care about you. I just wish you saw what I see in you and how much I wish you were mine instead of his. Don't feel guilty for something that we both wanted. And the next time anything is to go down between us, it's gonna' happen only if you ask me to." Chase never took his eyes away from mine as he spoke, and I heard the sincerity in his voice.

It didn't make me feel any better because when I answered Jayceon's call, I knew I'd have to lie to him. I didn't want to do that, but I had to.

"Let me help you the down the stairs, OK." Chase took my hand in his and helped me walk down the stairs to the parking lot.

"You good to drive?" He asked as he held the door open so I could get in.

I looked down at my ankle. The swelling had gone down a bit and it didn't hurt as much when I walked. "Yeah, I'll be aight." I started my engine because I couldn't wait to get the hell up out of there. I heard the sound of my phone vibrating again, and I knew it was Jayceon calling me back.

"Hey, don't let this be the last time I see your ass either. You heard me?"

"I hear you, Chase." Truth be told, I was never going to make myself available for this nigga again! I knew I couldn't trust myself around him. The physical attraction I felt was just too strong.

As I pulled out from the parking lot, I knew that I had to make it home in record time, or Jayceon may have jumped on a plane to come kill my ass. My world was about to come crashing down!

CHAPTER 25

*J*ayceon had called a total of five times by the time I got home, and I was pretty sure that he was frothing at the mouth. I planned to tell him that I was coming down with the flu and had took some medication that knocked me out. I hated to lie to him, but I couldn't exactly tell him that I was getting the life sucked out of my pussy from Chase!

As I stepped into the house, the nurse, Ms. Pearl, was walking out into the living room to meet me. I was about to say something to her but stopped when I saw the look on her face. I knew something was wrong.

"Shauntel." The way she said my name, and how she interlocked her fingers in front of her, let me know right then that my mother was gone.

I shook my head repeatedly, fell to a crumpled heap on the floor, and let out a heart-wrenching wail. "Noooooo, please no."

Ms. Pearl was at my side as she tried to lift me off the ground. "I'm so sorry, baby. I just went in to check on her a short while ago and found that God had called her home."

I hugged Ms. Pearl tightly as my body shook from silent sobs. My mother was gone. The only person that I had left was gone.

"She died peacefully, Shauntel. She went in her sleep. Would you like to go and view her body?"

I nodded and got up to walk to my mother's room. When I walked in, she lay with her hands on the sides of her body and looked like she was asleep. The tears rolled down my face as I walked over to her bed and lay my head on her lap. I recalled our last conversation before I left. It's like she knew her time was near and wanted me to know that she loved me.

"Mommy, please don't leave me," I said softly as I cried into her lap. Her body already felt cold.

My phone started ringing again. I looked at the screen, saw Jayceon's name, and answered.

"Yo, Shauntel. When I get back from Venezuela, remind a nigga to fuck you up for not answering your phone all those goddamn times that I been calling your ass." Hearing Jayceon's voice was so comforting even though he was yelling at me.

"Jayceon, she's gone." I was able to say that much before I started crying into the phone.

"Shaunie, baby, I'm on the first flight out of this bitch. I'm comin' home, baby."

*****

My mother's funeral was three days after her death. Jayceon was home first thing the next morning. I lay in bed, unable to sleep a wink. As soon as he opened my bedroom door, I literally crawled into his arms. He rocked me back and forth as he stroked my hair and said soothing words while I wept into the crook of his neck.

Jayceon was my rock for the days that led to her funeral. He handled the planning and also paid for everything. Lord knows, I had no strength to see about planning a funeral. Not to mention, Jayceon's birthday was in two days.

Chase hadn't tried to contact me since that night, and I was glad because the last thing I wanted to worry about was seeing him again anytime soon. Even though I was just as much to blame for what had happened between us, I was glad for the distance between us.

On the day of my mother's funeral, I felt like I was having an out of body experience. I sat at the front of the church with Jayceon at my side. The service was small because we didn't have many relatives. Jayceon's mother attended along with Jazmine. There was a big turnout on my father's side. They all hugged me and wished me well. I was just going through the motions. I could barely recall what was said to me or what I replied.

My mother looked like an angel as she laid in her coffin. She was at rest, and her pain was now gone. I gave her a final kiss goodbye.

"Shaunie, you gon' stay with me, and I don't wanna' hear any excuses. We'll swing by your crib and collect some of your things. Aight, bae," Jayceon said as we were leaving the cemetery after my mother's burial.

There was absolutely no need for me to argue with him. I mean, what was I going to go home to except an empty house filled with nothing but memories of my mother. "OK, Jay. that's fine," I said softly as he opened the door for me to get in to his Porsche. I sighed quietly as I buckled my seatbelt because I still had to somehow go through with celebrating Jay's birthday, which would be in the next two days.

At home, I went to my room and gathered a few clothes. Since I already had a lot of stuff at Jayceon's, I really didn't need much stuff. Next, I went into my mother's room and stood at the door. I stared at her bed. Knowing that I would never see her laying there anymore made my heart ache even more. The nurse we hired, Ms. Pearl, had helped me with packing my mother's clothes and belongings. We donated most of them to shelters.

As I felt myself began to tear up, Jayceon came behind me, placed his hands affectionately around my waist, and kissed the top of my head. "C'mon baby. If you got everything you need, let's go, aight."

I took one last look at her room as I walked to the front door with Jayceon. Then I took one last look around my home that I'd once shared with both my parents, which now just looked like an empty shell. I closed the door and locked it behind me. As I made my way to Jayceon's, I knew, in the back of my mind, that his place was about to be my new home.

After we got home, Jayceon ordered me to take a bath and go straight to bed. With Jayceon by my side, I was finally able to sleep for the first time in four days. With him lying next to me, I fell asleep in record time.

At about 10:00, there was a pounding at the front door, which caused me to jump out of my sleep. I looked at Jay, and he was still knocked out. I sat still and waited to make sure I heard correctly, and sure enough there was a knock again.

I shook Jayceon and tried to wake him. "Jay, baby. Wake up. There's somebody at the front door."

Jayceon stirred slightly. His eyes fluttered open slowly as I stared at him very agitatedly.

"Fuck, Shaunie, a nigga sleepy as a mothafucka. The fuck you waking me up for? What's wrong with you. You want me put it on you?" Jayceon said sleepily as his hand moved in between my legs.

I quickly knocked it away. "No, Jay. Listen, somebody's at the front door." As soon as those words passed my lips, there came an even louder knock than before.

"Whoever the fuck that is better hope I don't kill their mothafuckin' ass. Knockin' on my door all loud and shit." Jayceon got up, slipped a black pair of basketball shorts over his boxers, and pulled a white tee over his head as he made his way towards the door.

Curiosity got the better of me after a couple minutes passed and Jayceon hadn't returned to the bedroom. I slipped out of bed and made my way to the stairs wearing nothing but one of Jay's oversized sweatshirts.

While at the top of the stairs, I saw Jayceon standing with the door open with his hands crossed, speaking to someone that I couldn't see. It sounded like if he was answering questions, but I wasn't quite sure. So, I quietly started walking down the stairs, but stopped abruptly when I heard a voice coming from on the other side of the door. Something about that voice sounded very familiar.

"Man, you don't even have a fuckin' warrant, and you want me to let you come in here and illegally search my shit. Man, fuck you!"

With the mean mug Jayceon had on his face, I knew he was pissed off. I also knew that he was talking to a police officer by what he just said.

"Sir, we are going to have to place you under arrest."

What was it about that voice? I took one step further down the stairs because I'll be damned if they were just going to arrest my man for no reason whatsoever.

"Mothafucka'! Arrest me? For fuckin' what?" Jayceon took a step back as the officer took a step forward into the house with handcuffs in his hand.

I stood there looking at the uniformed officer with his handsome face, neatly trimmed goatee, and rich chocolate complexion. I almost shit in my drawers as Chase turned and saw me standing on the stairs.

You have got to be fucking kidding me!

If Chase was moved by my presence, I wouldn't have known because that nigga didn't even flinch. He then turned his attention back to Jayceon and said, "You were at a club a few weeks ago, and there was a double murder. We have you and your friends on camera outside of the club. We already have your friends, Maliq and Trevor in custody. So, we need to take you down to the station for questioning. We've also received an anonymous tip that you're hiding guns and ammunition at your house. As soon as we get a warrant, we'll be searching your premises."

I looked on in shock as Chase placed the handcuffs on Jayceon's wrists. "Chase, are you serious, right now? You're a cop?" I ran up to him and placed my hands on his arm as he continued putting the cuffs on Jay.

I saw a look of confusion on Jayceon's face as I said Chase's name, which made me realize that he didn't even recognize who Chase was.

"Shaunie, how the hell you know this fuck nigga?" Jay asked as he turned around and settled his angry gaze on me.

Before I could reply, Chase stood in front of Jayceon, took his police hat off, and smiled. "Oh, you don't remember me, nigga? You don't remember giving me this?" Chase turned around and displayed the scar that he had on the back of his head.

After a few seconds, Jayceon recognized the person that was arresting him, then started laughing hysterically.

"Yo, nigga. You a cop now? For real, for real? Man, get the fuck outta' here with all that bullshit. You still doing shit just to impress my girl? You must really like her, huh? Lookey here, take these mothafuckin' cuffs off my wrists then get the fuck out my crib, and I'll let you live to see another day. 'Cause what yo' dumb ass don't know, is that I got the law in my back pocket."

Chase and Jayceon stared at each other for about twenty seconds before Chase calmly put his hat back on and looked at the open front door.

It was only then that I realized another officer standing there. Chase signaled to him. "Go bring her in." Me and Jayceon watched. We were confused as the other officer, who looked to be about thirty years old, walked to the police car parked out front.

For the second time that night, I was left in shock because walking in with the officer was this stupid bitch, Nae Nae. The look on Jayceon's face as we watched as Nae Nae came and stood next to Chase, was that of complete rage. I saw it in his eyes when he looked at her.

"Is this the man that assaulted you, ma'am?" Chase asked Nae Nae as he pointed at Jay.

She nodded.

As I took a closer look, she actually did have a black eye. Now, who gave her that black eye, I had no clue. But I could be certain that it wasn't Jayceon. He never left my side since returning home from Venezuela. Jayceon rocked his head back. As he stared at Nae Nae's lying ass, his jaw clenched with rage.

"Bitch!" I roared as I lunged at Nae Nae. The other officer was quickly able to stand in between us before I could get my hands on her. I was almost certain that she was the *anonymous caller,* too.

"Aye, relax. Get her out of here," Chase said to his partner who quickly took hold of Nae Nae's upper arm and began leading her back to the car.

"Aye, Nae Nae," Jayceon called out to her.

She stopped and turned around.

"When I get out, you a dead bitch! You know how I do," Jayceon told her through clenched teeth. And for a split second, I saw fear in her eyes as the officer continued leading her away.

"Jayceon Clarke, you're under arrest. You have the right to remain silent . . ." Chase read Jayceon his Miranda Rights as he looked at me.

This had to be a dream, right? I mean, I'd just buried my mother, and now I was about to lose the only person I had left. On top of that, he was being taken away by somebody that I stupidly trusted.

"Aye, bruh. You don't want these problems when I get out. If I was you, I'd get the hell up out of dodge man. You have officially woken up the beast in me. It's alright, baby. I'll be home in no time." Jayceon winked and smiled at me as Chase began leading him out of the house.

I stood helplessly as Chase led Jayceon to a second police car. But not before he turned and looked at me. Honestly, I didn't even know how to feel towards Chase right now. I knew something was up from the way he kept dodging my question about what he did for a living. Why he chose to hide it, I had no idea.

What I did know was that Jayceon knew how to beat the system. I'd seen what he did for his little brother and how easy it was for him to get the charges against him dropped. I also knew that Jayceon didn't make idle threats. There was a war coming between Jayceon, Chase, and that dumb bitch, Nae Nae.

And unlike them, I knew my man was a straight savage.

TO BE CONTINUED

Looking for a publishing home?

Royalty Publishing House, Where the Royals reside, is accepting submissions for writers in the urban fiction genre. If you're interested, submit the first 3-4 chapters with your synopsis to submissions@royaltypublishinghouse.com.

Check out our website for more information: www.royaltypublishinghouse.com.

Text ROYALTY to 42828 to join our mailing list!

To submit a manuscript for our review, email us at submissions@royaltypublishinghouse.com

Text RPHCHRISTIAN to 22828 for our CHRISTIAN ROMANCE novels!

Text RPHROMANCE to 22828 for our INTERRACIAL ROMANCE novels!

Get LiT!

Download the LiTeReader app today and enjoy exclusive content, free books, and more

Do You Like CELEBRITY GOSSIP?

Check Out QUEEN DYNASTY!
Visit Our Site: www.thequeendynasty.com

CPSIA information can be obtained
at www.ICGtesting.com
Printed in the USA
LVOW03s0424190817
545584LV00017B/266/P

9 781973 918752